I0574125

PanTech Chronicles

BOOK ONE

SHADOWFALCON

F. LOCKHAVEN
M.A. OWENS

Editors
André MacLean
Katie Siciak
Grace Lockhaven

TWISTED KEY
p u b l i s h i n g
2024

First Printing: 2024

ISBN 978-1-63911-039-1

Twisted Key Publishing, LLC
www.twistedkeypublishing.com

Ordering Information:
Special discounts are available on quantity purchases by corporations, associations, educators, and others. For details, contact the publisher at the above listed address.

U.S. trade bookstores and wholesalers: Please contact Twisted Key Publishing, LLC by email twistedkeypublishing@gmail.com.

CONTENTS

I

I began to open my eyes reluctantly before changing my mind and tightening them shut again. Normally, I'd leap from my bed the moment consciousness became mine, but last night, unlike most nights, my dream had been something pleasant. When this happened, I liked to lie still and hope to fall back into it again, picking up where I left off. Not an exciting, action-packed adventure, or a romantic getaway with my dream guy, or counting my limitless wealth. No. In this dream, I was in a world alone. I rested on the baking hot sands outside my village, no bloodthirsty insects swarming my body to shower me in stings and bites, no shouts to take me from—

"Taylor, what are you doing? Get up. Your brother is already packed and ready!" The shout echoed both inside and outside of my mind. My beautiful mother stood over me when I wrenched apart my eyelids to look up at her. Well, beautiful on the outside at least, with her jet-black hair, narrow brown eyes, and skin far too pale to be suited for the desert. Her hair and her heart matched, I think, but I dare not say so.

"I'm up. It's the first time I've overslept in months, so cut me a break, huh?" I protested, though realizing I'd used up pointless oxygen in doing so no sooner than I'd finished the sentence.

"You haven't slept in. Your brother's just up early since he cares about making a good impression on others. You know that our guests are due any day now." She shoved her hand in my hair, her fingers getting stuck after just a few inches of brushing through. "You've been gifted with beauty, the best of both your father and I, and you can't even be bothered to take care of your hair." She pushed my head away roughly.

"Right, gotta look pretty for digging up terror ants and stitching up wounded pets. Thanks, Mother."

She frowned a deep, harsh frown that made her forehead wrinkle. "You never know who will walk by, or whose eye you'll catch when you return, or whose pet you're treating. If you fail your exam and get stuck here, your first goal should be to marry well."

I tensed. I'd gotten to hear this lecture several times a week for the past few years, and since I'd turned seventeen, almost every day. To say I was sick of it would be an understatement. At seventeen, I was already our village's veterinarian. I'd become an apprentice at fourteen and should've studied for ten years, but my teacher died suddenly of a stroke a few months ago, leaving me to take over and the apprentice who'd started a year later than me, Cara, to become my apprentice. I could take care of myself.

At one time, my father had been a renowned inventor and teacher, but our…'guests,' as Mother liked to call them, had put a stop to that. His inventions interfered with our village's adversity rating because they made everyone's lives easier, and he was warned that if he continued, they would have to raise the threshold for passing the exams, something our 'guests' came by to administer yearly and allowed every eighteen-year-old the opportunity to be selected for service by PanTech, and leave the adversity zone. Father became more and more bitter. It was hard to be around him nowadays. Even the most minor accident would send him into a tirade of expletives and combinations of expletives. Sometimes new ones, as though he was determined to at least be able to continue inventing something.

"Okay," I said to my mother, taking a deep breath. "I'll comb my hair. Now, could I have some privacy? I'd like to get dressed, so my dear brother doesn't have to keep waiting." I felt a tinge of guilt hit me the moment I finished the sentence. It was meant to be a sarcastic remark to irritate Mother, but my brother had always been good to me. Better than anyone else had, at least, even though he was a fool and a coward without equal. Well, except for maybe Mother, with her 'guests', and 'we should be thankful' and all of her phrases that made Father's face contort into shapes that might resemble a volcano if it were trying desperately not to erupt despite desperately wanting to…if volcanos were human, I guess.

"Good. Maybe try speaking a bit more lady-like too. I know you think you're above it because you've been lucky in life, but if you are fortunate enough to experience greater adversity, your beauty and your manners may be all you have. Sharpen them while you can."

I rubbed my forehead, wondering if my face was taking on the strange, furious, involuntary shapes my father's did when she said things like this to him. I hoped I had better self-control than he did in that respect. "You're right, of course. Thank you for your advice." I opened the door, encouraging her to leave as politely but as quickly as I thought she'd let me away with. Thankfully, it worked. She sighed, nodded to me, and stepped quickly through the door, which I promptly closed behind her, calling up every ounce of my will not to slam it so hard it exploded into ten thousand splinters. At least, that's what I imagined it would do if I could manage to convert my irritation directly into physical strength.

Closing the door left me staring into the mirror that hung from it, cracked, from the times I hadn't been able to summon that willpower. Maybe I'd inherited my temperament from my father, the way my brother did from our mother. I'd inherited his dark skin as well, but unfortunately not his hair and eyes. Every time I looked into this mirror, I saw a darker-skinned version of Mother, looking back at me and judging me for being such a disappointment. I'm not sure why I cared. Would Mother really be happy if I put on makeup, spent an hour brushing my hair, and walked around town pretending to struggle with carrying some tiny something until a handsome, rich boy tore it from my hands, steadied me on my feet, and kissed me deeply before promising I'd never want for anything ever again? My cheeks warmed a little at the thought, but I snapped back into reality, scolding myself for getting caught up in the scene that played out in my mind. Stupid imaginary handsome stranger and his perfect kissing technique, muscled arms, and long wavy hair blowing in the desert wind. Grrr! I'll punch him in the face if I ever see him…maybe. I shook my head violently and slammed my open hands into my cheeks. *Pull it together, Taylor.*

I threw open my closet doors. My tiny wardrobe of highly practical and very unladylike outfits filled the tiny space, including the very unpretty one I designed to slow down a terror ant attack in the case that my latest technique of harvesting their hives didn't work or didn't work well enough. It was more of a psychological trick I played on myself than anything else. After all, it only took a few terror ant bites to leave you hunched over a bucket for days heaving out your guts and wishing your mother had never given birth to you in the first place, or that you could at least swap pains with her in the process. There was nothing quite like a terror ant bite. I was tempted to describe it as a hot nail being driven into the skin, but that would stop hurting after a few moments, whereas the terror ant's bite didn't for days. The tingling and numbness lasted weeks, sometimes months, in older bite victims. The lucky ones, that is. More than a few bites would land you in the grave. Your hollow bones, at least. They made quick work of everything else. I had to give my brother credit for being willing to go out and do this with me. Bravery and stupidity are siblings, my father used to say. It ended up being an ironic statement in his case.

I threw on the outfit and flung open my door before realizing I had forgotten to comb my hair. I quickly closed it again and spent the next few seconds brushing my comb through my hair painfully, completely disregarding the 'proper' technique my mother showed me. I didn't have all morning, after all. Correction, the morning was all I had. Once it became light out, the terror ants were more active, and this would be suicide. It could be regardless, but we could at least take the proper precautions to put the odds in our favor. A terror ant hive was such a delicacy to PanTech's proper citizens that it could supply my clinic and feed my family for weeks. Apparently, you could only find them here, or so I guessed. It's not like we knew anything about the other adversity zones. Or how many there were. We assume that there must be several, considering we didn't recognize any of the employees who came by to check in our cozy little village to ensure our adversity level was still optimal. For our own good, of course.

My second attempt to leave my room worked out better. Just outside my door, rounding the corner, was the common room where my mother was preparing food. My brother was sitting at the table, a small piece of meat on his plate. He'd remembered my instructions, at least. If you ate a full meal while trying to wear these clothes, things would get unbearably tight very quickly. The longest I'd ever been able to wear it when testing it was a few hours, and by then, you're up against prolonged restricted breathing or a heat stroke, both of which were preferred death to terror ant bites. "Thanks for being ready," I offered. "We'd better get going."

My father's attention was held by a mess of papers on the large wooden table, glancing over them while finishing a long puff on his smoking pipe. Preparing the upcoming school year's curriculum in something, I suppose. He was brilliant, so it could've been anything. But, aside from my brother and I, he didn't have the heart to teach anymore. "I still think you're crazy for doing this, Tay, and even crazier for dragging your poor brother along. When you get back, I'll need you to deliver these to the school. I'm nearly done now, so I expect I'll be done with them by then." He never looked up at us or took his eyes off his papers. He only took another long pull from his pipe and blew out a cloud of smoke that filled the air with a pleasant cactus berry aroma. Father was clever with language. It was frowned upon to offer your children too many kind or encouraging words. It would affect their adversity, after all, to have parents who were too kind. But, in that one simple phrase, implying he expected us to be back soon, what he'd really said was, *You're brave. I believe in you. You'll succeed, and I'll see you soon.*

"Sure, I'll drop them off on my way to the clinic," I said. "Ferris, are you ready?"

"Born ready. Born ready to get this suit off as soon as possible, at least," Ferris replied, wiggling uncomfortably in his chair.

I sighed. "If you're going to start complaining this early, you're going to really love it when we start walking around in them. Or when you have to put the mask on. Or when the first terror ant crawls—"

"Okay! I get it. Try not to be too grateful. You'll hurt yourself." His tone said he meant it as an insult, but his smile said the opposite. Only I saw the smile.

"Alright, you two need to leave. I have work to do," Father said. "You said you needed the cooler morning air before the sunrise for this to be safest, so you better get going." *Good luck*, he was most likely thinking.

I took a deep breath, or at least what would have to substitute for a deep breath, grabbed my rucksack with the supplies I needed next to the door, and lit our lantern. I stopped just before opening the door and took a long look around. I was probably crazy for doing this, and who knew what my brother was thinking. The two of us looked at each other. I placed my hand on the door handle for a long moment, my way of offering him one last chance to change his mind. He didn't.

We flung open the door and ventured out into the dark, open desert to tempt fate for profit.

2

"Did we really have to cover ourselves in that nasty-smelling meat grease?" Ferris whispered behind me.

"No. I mean, you didn't have to. It would take you all day to get the suit on, and your sweat would attract the ants. Be my guest and try something different next time," I replied at my normal volume, making no effort to mask my irritation at even being asked such a stupid question.

"Alright, sheesh. You're the expert. I'm just making conversation." He whispered, as though he couldn't help himself but be polite, even in the dark when no one else was likely to hear him.

"Well...," I started, "you could try asking useful questions. Like maybe ask me why I chose to use the grease instead of any one of the many more pleasant oils Mother keeps around the house. You could also ask me why the sugar water line in the sand works to draw them from their nest. You could ask—"

"You're scared, aren't you? Me too," he offered, whispering even more quietly this time, his tone softening. He was the only person who could make me angry and remind me why I loved him in the span of a few seconds. Well, aside from Father, when he had one of his verbal tirades. It was hard to tell at a glance that we were brother and sister. His hair was rough, like Father's, and he kept it tied in a tight ponytail. His skin was a softer brown, much closer to Mother's, and he had Father's emerald green eyes. He also had Father's natural affinity for language. If he said the wrong thing, he knew the right thing to say to instantly make it better, no matter who he was speaking to. He hadn't lost his temper and started shouting foul language for all the village to hear. At least, not yet. Maybe that would happen when he got older like they say it did with Father.

"You...," I started to say, in my usual snappy tone I often took with him, that he rarely deserved. I took a breath and started again. "You're right...I'm sorry. I'm a little on edge. And yeah, I'm a little scared. Have you ever seen a body swarmed by terror ants?"

"Unfortunately...yeah, I have."

"And you still came?" I laughed nervously.

"I know *you* have, and you're still going."

We both went quiet and continued to walk through our dark village by the dim lantern light. We could see not a single toy or a sign that children existed. They were carefully hidden away indoors. I'd heard of some parents going as far as hiding them in the walls or under the floor's stone. Mother forbade them in our house, but Father always found a way to sneak things to us that *technically* weren't toys. I remembered the first doll he made for me. Anatomy reference, as he called it. You're never too young to study the human body, especially if you may have a future in medicine. Of course, it turned out that I would be interested in medicine, but the doll I just played with in my room. After he'd given me another, I made them talk to each other quietly. I still remember the day Mother caught me by listening through my door and meant to throw them into the fire. Father managed to stop her. He told her it was an exercise he'd given me to simulate human interaction in the role of a physician trying to diagnose a patient. There was no point in facing adversity as a child if you were too uneducated to be of use to PanTech.

That was when he still pretended, of course. When he was still trying to appease Mother. Now, he rarely did. He'd call PanTech every name in the book and say he didn't care if they executed him, before he'd finally calm down and return to his work as though nothing ever happened.

I shook my head vigorously, flinging the thoughts from my mind. The last thing I needed was for my head to be in the clouds. "I use the grease from rotten meat because the stench slows down the ants. They like sweat and sweet smells. Sweat is how they target their prey. They aren't scavengers, so if you smell rotten, they think twice before swarming you. It buys you a little time if you rile them up. Not long. A few seconds at best before they do…whatever it is they do to determine you are, in fact, alive and swarm you anyway. I've tested this with animal carcasses. Sometimes they hesitate as long as five seconds. And, of course, these suits are too tight to get into otherwise."

"Ah, right, that makes sense. That explains the sugar water too," Ferris said, in his normal voice, I assume accidentally. He snapped his head around quickly to make sure no one had heard him and might be upset that he'd disturbed them. This is something I did not like about my brother. He was good at making everyone like him, but he cared far too much about whether or not they did.

"See, you're getting it. Now we just have to not die. I saw a hive not far from here, just out of sight of the village that needed to be dealt with anyway. Do you remember how to put the rest on?"

He started to twist to see inside his pack but realized he wouldn't easily be able to and just swung the pack around in front of him instead. He pilfered through it a moment. "Gloves, mask, wraps to cover the gaps. We're going to roast in these, Taylor."

I nodded. "Yep, if we drag our feet," I said, slowing my pace. "It should be around here somewhere. We have to be careful not to get too close. We need to stop just at the edge of the lantern light."

I wished now that I'd practiced more with spotting these in the dark by dim light. If we accidentally stepped on a hive, we'd be dead by the time we realized the ants bit us. Figures I'd overlook a detail *that* important....

"We have to be getting close," I said. Now I was the one whispering. "We're taking baby steps from here on out. Help me look for them. There's usually one or two nearby, even at night." I squinted and looked side to side as I walked, mere inches with each step. "I don't see anything yet." Suddenly, Ferris grabbed my arm hard. I turned to see what had alarmed him, but he didn't speak. He only pointed. I followed his finger's direction and saw one of the little demons crawling just at the edge of the light. "We'll put our hat and gloves on. You go first. I'll watch it. They never spend more than a few minutes out of the hive before switching guard with a new ant."

"Got it." He opened his pack, pulled out the gloves, and began working them on, taping them up at the small overlap at the wrist, before struggling several minutes with the hat. "Nice thinking with the mesh hood. I'm not sure how we could get bit through this thick leather either."

"Don't be so sure…," I said. "Keep an eye on it." Once I completed my suit, I took one more look up to the sky. Good, still pitch dark.

"Over there," he said, pointing a few feet from where I'd last seen the ant. "I saw it crawl into the hive over there, after another crawled out."

I dropped my pack on the ground, pulling out two small clay bowls and a large bottle filled with sugar water. "Stay here," I whispered. "I have to isolate that one, quickly. Get the shovel ready. Remember, right along the lines of the water. Hard, just along the edge, then throw it aside. Three good times should do it, then run like your life depends on it. It does."

He nodded, bent down, and started connecting the two parts of his shovel. I began to drag my feet toward the ant hive in even, smooth motions. In my previous experiments, I'd found that stepping alerted them the quickest. The vibrations underground set them off. Things sliding along the surface of the sand alerted them much more slowly. I stopped a foot or so away from the ant, swallowed hard, and brought the bowl down as quickly as I could, trapping the ant beneath. I dragged the bowl a few feet further from the nest, pushed it down into the sand, and let go. After a few tense moments of watching the nest open, I pulled the top from the bottle and began pouring the water in a narrow line a few inches from the nest's opening, on the side opposite Ferris and I. I went back and forth for a moment until the bottle was finally emptied. I threw it back toward Ferris, and he caught it, tossing my second bowl toward me, which I also caught. I slid my feet back a few steps and waited for the second ant to cycle out. What was taking so long?

I glanced back to Ferris, who shrugged his shoulders. I held up my hand, signaling for him to wait or be calm, but maybe I was projecting my own nervousness. They usually didn't take this long to come out. Did something go wrong with the water? Too much sugar? Not enough?

On top of everything else, I'd begun sweating profusely, which just added to my anxiety. Finally, an ant popped out and was immediately distracted by the sugary water pooled on top of the sand. Again, I did the same thing, capturing it under my bowl and pulling it over next to the other. I stood next to them for a moment, watching the opening. I held up my hand, ready to signal Ferris. Counting in my head.

Nineteen, eighteen, seventeen, sixteen.

I slid my feet back, slowly making my way back toward Ferris.

Fifteen, fourteen, thirteen, twelve.

I held up my hand, looking at him over my shoulder. He gripped the shovel tightly and nodded.

Eleven, ten, nine, eight.

I bent down, sliding my bottle back into my pack.

Seven, six, five, four.

I picked up my pack with my free hand, sliding it off one shoulder.

Three, two, one.

I brought my hand down in a sharp motion, and Ferris sprinted toward the nest, burying the shovel into the ground, then turning out the sand beside him. One down. He plunged the shovel down a second time. The angle was too sharp. No!

Ants swarmed out of the hive in all different directions.

"Drop it and run!" I screamed.

He tossed the sand aside and plunged the shovel down a third time.

"I said drop it, idiot! Forget it!"

The third shovel went in smoothly, and he turned up the hive, roughly the size of a human head. Ants were already swarming onto the shovel from the nest and would be all over him soon after.

"Drop it and run!" I shouted to the very limits of my voice, even though he was just a few feet away from me. This time, at least, he listened. He threw the shovel aside and bolted in my direction. I grabbed his pack from the ground and tossed it toward him before turning myself. We wouldn't have to sprint far. Just enough to get out of their range. We'd still be able to see the hive, but terror ants lost interest quickly beyond a certain distance.

After a few seconds of running, I stopped and looked over my shoulder. They'd stopped following us and instead swarmed around the nest with all the fury that comes with having your home unearthed when you were one of the most dangerous insects in the desert. They wanted something to pay.

"They'll swarm around for the morning, but they'll abandon the hive by noon," I said in my calmest voice before turning and punching him with everything I had in his shoulder.

"Ouch, what was that for?" he shouted, jumping back.

"Stupid! Stupid!" I screamed, punching him again, and drew back to hit him again before freezing in place. "Oh no…don't move. Don't even breathe."

He knew what that meant, and he became a statue. There was an ant on his shoulder…and another on his leg. I drew back my open hand and smashed the one on his shoulder.

He shrieked a full second later. At first, I thought I'd hit him too hard, but then I realized….

"Stay calm. Don't move!" I said, circling him to get a better angle on the ant on his leg. It bit through the leather!

"Get it! Get it!" He was trembling now, and his voice gave away the tears. Fear, or pain, both of which were understandable. I dropped to my knees and quickly swatted it before it could bite again.

"Let me check the rest of you. You stupid, stupid idiot!"

"It burns. Oh, man. I'm going to die." His trembling intensified.

I didn't want to think about it, but there had been villagers who died from a single bite, but none of them as big as my brother.

"You're not going to die," I said, still looking him over. "Okay. Okay…I think that's it. Next time when I say to drop the shovel, drop it!" I yelled, suppressing the urge to punch him again.

"I…," he began speaking but didn't continue, starting to sway. His head lowered.

"Ferris?"

His head snapped back up again. "I don't think I can walk with my leg. I can't feel it. Go get help."

I eyed the rising sun. As much as I loved the sun, I hated the sight of it now. I dropped my pack and ripped off my hat and gloves. "There's no time. Between the bite and the heat, you'll be dead before I make it back. Drop your pack. We have to beat the sunlight. Climb on my back."

"No, Tay. It's too far. That'll kill you too. Just go."

"Now!" I shouted, punching him again in the shoulder, though I held back a little this time.

He winced, though I knew it wasn't from me. I ripped off his hat and turned my back to him, kneeling.

"Ferris, hurry."

We stood there like that a moment in a stalemate of stubbornness, but he finally gave in, collapsing onto my back. Could I actually carry him all the way back? I could barely stand up with him. He was so much bigger than me. No. No, I would have to. I'd have to find a way.

I stared into the distance toward our village, not even in sight, my body already feeling like it was roasting beneath the breaking dawn. I wrapped my arms behind his knees and cried out as I shrugged to my feet. I gritted my teeth, closed off my mind from the heat and the pain, and took my first steps.

3

I had the same dream again, lying on the hot desert sands, not a sound other than the light breeze passing over me. I stretched my limbs, grabbing handfuls of sand and letting it fall between my fingers. I was startled this time when I looked up and saw Ferris there. He was standing there, smiling, the wind blowing through his hair. I smiled back and tried to speak to him, but no sound escaped my mouth.

"You did this," he said, still smiling.

I tried to answer, but again, I couldn't speak.

"You did this," he repeated.

I panicked, grabbing my throat. I tried to stand but couldn't sit up. Ants swarmed up around me, but they passed over me, climbing up Ferris's legs, then his torso.

"You did this," he said again.

No, I wanted to scream. *I'm sorry,* is what I should have tried to say.

The ants bit at him ferociously, tearing his skin, but still, he smiled at me.

"You did this."

I opened my mouth to scream, but there was nothing. Finally, my voice came to me, as well as my strength. I bound up from the desert floor with a shriek, but something grabbed me—something I couldn't see.

"Tay...," the voice was distant. Muffled.

I fought again to get free, screaming for Ferris to run.

"Tay!" The voice was closer this time. Father?

"Tay! Calm down. I'm here. You're alright," came his voice, like sunbeams piercing a deep dark abyss. The desert faded around me.

"Father? I'm sorry...I thought I...Where's Ferris?" I shouted.

"Try to calm yourself. You're delirious from the heat. You must take water. Sit, please," my father pleaded as he offered me an open canteen.

I sat back onto my bed and took the water from him, drinking it with a thirst I hadn't felt in as long as I could remember. I finished the entire thing in less than half the time it should have taken.

"Ferris. Is he okay?" I said more calmly this time.

"He is. He's not as tough as you, but he's tougher than you realize. He woke up about an hour ago, much in the way you did, raving about his sister." He laughed at this, for some reason. "Gather yourself, and go see him. I'm sure he already heard your screaming and knows you're awake."

I nodded. I'm sure he did. I was so unbelievably embarrassed for screaming in front of Father like that. I lowered my head and smelled my arm, then pulled my hair in and inhaled deeply, looking up at him with my eyebrows narrowed.

"Your mother," he said, pulling the unspoken question from my mind. I wasn't sure whether I should be thankful or angry. My hair was expertly combed and shampooed with the same fragrances Mother always used. My hands were soft with scented lotions, and I had a sinking feeling she'd put makeup on me, but when I leaned to the side so that I could see the mirror on my door, I was relieved to see that she at least hadn't gone that far.

I touched my face and sighed.

Father gave me a firm slap on the shoulder. "For once, I agreed with your mother. We could smell you coming before we saw you," he said with a broad smile. "Come. You seem to be feeling well enough." He gave me his hand and helped me stand. I still felt sick from the heat, and my memory was still a haze.

I looked down and sighed again. "Such a beautiful dress Mother has put me in," I said sarcastically.

"It is," he agreed, but without a hint of sarcasm, before motioning for me to follow him. I did.

Around the corner from my room was Ferris's. As Father pushed open the door, I saw Mother and our village doctor applying a salve to his wound.

"Knock, next time," the giant man growled. If you had any number of guesses as to what Doc Norman's profession was, solely based on appearance, you certainly wouldn't guess that he was a doctor. His beard was larger and thicker than Father's but just as white. Father wasn't a small man, but Doc Norman stood a full head taller, with broader shoulders and a barrel chest.

"Sorry, Doc," I said in my most ladylike voice I could muster. I didn't want my father flying off the handle and getting into an argument with Doc while tending to Ferris. "Thank you for tending to Ferris." Father raised a brow, but Mother looked as though she would explode with pride. This surprised me. I couldn't remember Mother ever looking at me that way, and it hurt. It also made me regret that I'd spoken that way just to save Father's blood pressure. Then again, maybe that's what she was impressed with. She'd been telling me more lately that I needed to use my feminine gifts to persuade and stop behaving like I was her second son. Remembering that, the warm feeling that was there for only a moment quickly faded.

"Sorry indeed," Doc grumbled. "You should be caned for dragging your brother out there so—"

"I dragged him back too, didn't I?" I interrupted in my regular tone.

"Yes. So you nearly got Ferris killed, but you also saved his life. I hope you don't show that same kindness to my wife's spike-head lizard when she brings him to see you tomorrow."

"Your wife's spike-head lizard will probably follow my instructions better."

He looked down at Ferris and grunted. Or it could've been a laugh. Just about everything sounded like a grunt with Doc. "That I can believe." He looked to my mother, holding up the canister he'd scooped the salve from. "Twice a day for pain. I can do nothing for the healing, but that will happen on its own. He's young and strong."

She bowed her head. "Thank you, Doctor."

"Yes, thank you," Father added.

We stood silently for a moment before Father jabbed me with his elbow and cleared his throat.

I bowed my head. "Thank you, and please send my regards to your wife," I said, in my sweeter voice again. I could practically feel Mother beaming from where she sat on my brother's bed.

Suddenly, Ferris's arm shot up from the bed, pointing at me. "What has that feminine creature done to my sister?"

I gritted my teeth. "Shut up," I shouted. "I should've left you out there to feed the ants!" I turned quickly, outpacing my father's arm that had reached out to grab for me, and slammed the door behind me. I ran to my room and slammed that door, too, causing the mirror to fall off and shatter onto the floor before I could catch it. I put my hands over my mouth, sat on my bed, and started sobbing quietly. Why did I react that way? I hated when I lost my temper that way. He was clearly joking, and I knew he had to be in so much pain, even with Doc's salve. He was trying to make me laugh. It was Mother I was angry with, not him. But...I wasn't sure she deserved it either.

A knock came. "Tay." Father's voice.

"Just a minute."

"Come to the table when you're ready. I need to speak with you."

I didn't answer, just wiped my face with my sleeves and sniffed before climbing onto the floor and picking up the pieces of glass. I had intended to come in here and change, but now that I'd calmed down, I thought better of it. I had doubled my appointments yesterday so I could retrieve the hive today without a limit on time.

Time.

Time?

Time!

It was already past noon, surely. It would spoil if it stayed out any longer. I dropped the glass onto the table beside my bed and rushed from the room toward the front door.

"Tay," Father said firmly.

I stopped short of the door. "I'm sorry. I'll be back. I have to get the hive before it spoils!" I reached out and grabbed the handle.

"Stop!" he shouted.

"I said I'm sorry. I'll be back soon."

"It's late in the day. It would've been too late," he said.

"Oh no! Wait…*would've* been?"

He smiled and reached under the table, pulling out a large sphere wrapped in cloth.

I clapped my hands together and ran over to him, hugging his neck tightly.

He chuckled with surprise. "Aren't you glad I was so nosey when you explained all of this to your brother?"

"You're the best," I said genuinely.

"Me? Who said anything about me?" He said, raising his brow.

"You don't mean…," I said, my eyes widening.

"Don't you think you should—"

"Apologize? Probably…."

He narrowed his eyes at me.

I sighed. "Absolutely. Definitely. Big time."

I stood up straight when Doc walked up to us, and he stood in front of me, grabbing my head roughly, taking the other hand to pull up one of my eyelids. He placed the back of his hand on my cheek, then grabbed my hand and looked at my fingernails.

"Light sweating. Normal skin. Fingernails are showing signs of dehydration," I said.

Doc grunted. "You may behave like an animal sometimes, Taylor, but you're a human, or so your parents keep insisting. I'm the human doctor." He patted me on the head. "Get some rest, and drink as much water as you can keep down. Don't exert yourself anymore today."

He stepped out the door without another word.

I looked to Father. "Unwrap it," I said.

"The hive?"

"Yes. Can you think of a grander apology?"

"Guess not, but the chieftain pays by weight, doesn't he?"

I nodded. "It's alright. It'll just be a thin slice. Just enough for a taste."

He unfolded the cloth with a noticeable reluctance. I pulled a knife from a nearby drawer and slowly, very carefully, took a thin slice off the top. It was bright yellow and spongy, making a crackling noise as the knife slid back and forth. As I sliced, Father grabbed two plates.

"Four," I said, correcting him. "You better believe we're getting a taste too."

He went back and fetched two more plates, setting them close to the hive on the table.

"PanTech soldiers call this cake the 'Miracle of the Desert,'" I said to him as I finished the slice, balancing it carefully on the knife.

"Hmph!" He shrugged his shoulders. "I hope they eat an ant."

"The ants leave it," I said before pausing. "But, we can hope."

Placing the slice on one plate, I split it into four and divided it amongst the plates, picking up two of them.

"Grab the other two," I said before heading toward my brother's room and flinging open the door.

"Tay, I just wanted to say—" Ferris started.

"Sorry," I said, both cutting him off and, I realized, finishing his sentence. "I should be able to take a joke. Here, I thought we should have a taste before I take it to the chieftain." I handed a plate to him and Mother, then turned and took one from Father.

Ferris was the first to take a bite. "Woah! Totally worth getting bit by a terror ant. How can those evil things make something that tastes like this?"

Mother brought her piece to her lips, sliding it gently into her mouth.

"Well, I've found they like sweet things. I think they somehow refine it inside their body and condense the sugars over and over before regurgitating it into their nest material. Creates a flavor even PanTech hasn't been able to reproduce, apparently."

For a moment, I thought Mother would gag. She paused, but placing manners above all else, quickly resumed chewing before smiling. "Amazing. It's no wonder our guests love this so much."

Father winced, and I was afraid he was about to lose his temper, but he looked at me, grabbed the piece from his plate, and tossed it into his mouth. "It's good. Too good for them," he said.

Mother shook her finger at him. "Please don't say things like that. I've told you. What if someone hears you?"

"Let them hear me!" he shouted. "What more can they take from me? They already took my life's work."

"Your family. Your children's futures. We should be grateful to them. Living in adversity makes us better. It makes us strong."

He threw up his arms in frustration. "This again?"

I sighed, taking the piece from my plate, biting off half of it and chewing it slowly. I'd put all that work into scavenging for these in the past before I developed the extraction method, but not once had I tasted one. It was heavenly. It was like a cake, but a thousand times sweeter. The flavor seemed to melt into my tongue and didn't diminish as I held it there. I wondered for a moment how long a human could go without swallowing, but several shouts from outside our home startled me and I swallowed hard.

"They're here!" one said.

"Go and get changed. You'll want to look your best," another shouted.

Mother smiled. "Best you run as quickly as you can to get the rest of this to the chieftain so that he can present it to our guests."

I had been dreading this day for weeks.

4

I quickly rewrapped the hive on the table and made for the door, barely slowing to turn the handle and spill out into the open world. Or at least what we were allowed to experience of the open world. PanTech decided just how open it was allowed to be. A wall encircled the entire area, several miles out from the village. I'd walked along its edges many times. It wasn't a wall that could be destroyed, or scaled, or even seen. Markers jutted from the sand to show where the invisible wall ran. Anything that wasn't human could pass through it, but if a human tried, they were pushed back and paralyzed temporarily. Father said that when he was younger, a boy had actually managed to run through it, so they modified it. Now, the effect started much sooner and became so strong that you would be completely incapacitated or dead long before you could sprint through it. "We knew that," he had said, "because a few still tried."

People like my mother didn't seem to understand that. I didn't care if adversity made me a better person. Maybe it did, but shouldn't I decide? Was I really expected to appreciate soldiers, our so-called 'guests,' to come by and make sure we didn't have too much food, or that people like Father hadn't found a way to make our lives easier, or people like me hadn't—

I shook my head, discarding the thought. I wasn't aware of any way they had of reading minds, but they had ways of knowing things that we often couldn't figure out. I focused my mind on what was in front of me.

Our home was almost on the other side of the village from the chieftain, so I would have to ignore the urge to vomit I had building in my stomach. I should have taken water with me, but in my haste, I'd forgotten. As I jogged through the village, most people outside moved in the opposite direction toward the village. I dodged and weaved through dead eyes and barely-beating hearts. They couldn't wait to see their masters and get their pat on the head. I was nearly knocked down by an elderly woman who rounded a corner at the same time as me as I finally made it in sight of the chieftain's home. She fell onto her back, dropping the basket of clothes she was carrying.

"Oh no! I'm sorry. Here, let me help you." I wrapped one arm under hers and helped her to her feet. I expected to get an earful, but she only chuckled.

"My, I guess my granddaughter was right about something exciting happening in the village."

"Aren't you going to go and see them?" I asked.

"Why? Are they going to help me with my laundry?"

"Never know. They might. They only seem to care about making your life harder if you're under eighteen or if you're making the life of someone under eighteen easier."

"Well then," she said, chuckling again. "It looks like they'll be glad I stepped out in front of you and almost made you fall. Don't worry about me, dear. Worry about yourself. You speak far too freely for a girl your age. You'll be safer keeping thoughts like that to yourself."

She was right, of course.

"I really have to be going. I'm sorry for running into you."

She waved her hand dismissively and gave me a push from behind. I bowed slightly, then ran the rest of the way to the chieftain's house, where he was waiting outside.

The chieftain was one of the only overweight men in the village, and I was convinced that PanTech had selected him specifically because they knew he would do a lousy job. In fact, that was almost a given, considering they punished adults for improving the youth's lives in any way. It was rare for him to be willing to pay for something like this, but he knew how much the soldiers loved their 'Miracle of the Desert,' and he leaped at the chance to kiss their feet.

He frowned at me when he noticed me arrive. "I thought you were coming earlier. Well, that will surely reduce your price-uh," he said, without giving me time to answer, turning to walk around behind his very nice house where he kept his scale, waving for me to follow.

The way he spoke annoyed me far more than anything about the way he looked like he was trying to change his accent deliberately so he wouldn't sound like the rest of us. The premise, of which, was so idiotic it was hard to be believed. The village is isolated. Where else exactly could he have come from? Aside from that, he was the son of the last village chieftain, so there really was no doubt. If you got him flustered enough, he'd revert to his usual way of speaking, but otherwise, he'll add this strange 'uh' sound to the end of a lot of his words. I also didn't like how he looked at the other girls in the village or me. At all. I found myself wishing I'd taken the time to change into my more practical clothes after all.

I handed him the hive carefully, and he placed it on the scale. "So, we're down from three hundred marks per pound to two hundred fifty," he said, shaking his head, as though he was disappointed in having to rip me off.

"Uh-huh," I said, still hoping to salvage the situation in some diplomatic way. What I'd rather do is pull out my knife and stick it in his neck, but as I have been told repeatedly lately, I was a lady now, and that would be very unladylike behavior.

"What would you say this paper weighs-uh...several ounces I'd imagine-uh."

"Not even an ounce," I said, crossing my arms.

"Right. Five ounces from the look of it-uh."

He peeled back the paper. "What's this? Did you take a slice-uh from it?"

I cocked my head. "What difference would that make? But no," I lied. "I did no such thing. It was like that when I pulled it from the sands."

"I see-uh. Remind me, how did you tell me you extracted it?"

"I didn't."

We were quiet for the next few moments. I hoped he was just as worried about me as I was about him. Even at two hundred fifty marks per pound, that would still keep the clinic and my home going for weeks if I really stretched it.

"Mmm, I don't believe you-uh. Two hundred marks per pound. It is both late and...damaged-uh." He wrinkled his nose and sniffed, then coughed without covering his mouth.

"With all due respect, sir, you won't be ready in time if we take much longer. I'd heard that our guests were making their way straight here first," I lied again.

I noticed that he'd taken his hand that had been down at his side and placed it on the table, curling his fingers under the bowl of the scale, lifting it ever so slightly to remove several ounces from the weight. "Right-uh. Let's see then. It looks like…umm…."

I rolled my eyes. "Sir, it looks like you accidentally moved up against the scale. You'd better take a step back while it settles on a number; otherwise it may add extra weight. I wouldn't want you to overpay."

He curled his lip. "Right-uh…," he backed a step away. We watched the number for a moment, and when the hand of the scale stopped moving, he turned and started dropping the small copper marks into a small sack, with his back facing me…of course. After a minute of clinging and clanging into the sack, he tied a string around it tightly, no doubt to discourage me from counting. The chieftain had plenty of money to spare. He no longer had to worry about his own adversity, and as long as someone was as self-centered as he was, PanTech couldn't care less. He certainly wasn't doing anything to make anyone's life more comfortable around here. You couldn't make him want to do that if you held a knife to his throat.

I took the sack from him. "Thanks. By the way, I spent weeks finding this one. They're getting to be rare. Probably going to need at least four hundred per pound next time."

"Four hun—" he shouted before stopping himself and lowering his voice again. "Four hundred per pound. Are you out of your mind?"

"No, and it was a lot of work carrying all of the gear out there and back, preparing it for transport, and getting it to you in time to present it to our guests. I also had to close my clinic today. I'm thinking about adding a delivery fee." I scratched my chin. "But you're a much more experienced businessman than I am. What do you think?"

He took a deep breath that sounded more like a wheeze. "Girl, I have ways of making sure your life here gets a lot harder, so you may not want to play that game with me."

He wasn't lying. He could, and PanTech would pat him on the back for it. *More adversity will make her better. You've done well*, they'd say.

I held up the sack. "I know you mean what you say. So do I. Good day to you, sir."

I bowed my head, turned, and left a little quicker than is customary, but I didn't want to give him time to think of whatever kind of sick thing he probably wanted to say. I hoped he wouldn't even ask me to get another hive for him. I'd improve the clinic going some other way. If Mother were here, she'd have been disappointed in me for disrespecting the chieftain that way and being so impulsive...why did I even care?

I made it almost back to our house when I bumped into someone again, my mind still in the clouds, worried the chieftain might retaliate.

"Hello," the voice said simply.

I'd stumbled backward and taken a moment to gather myself and look up. Standing before me was one of the PanTech soldiers. A handsome one, too, maybe a few years older than me. Shoulder-length blonde hair with bright blue eyes, and pale skin. Even more so than Mother's.

"I'm...," I choked on my words. Is he angry? You don't usually say hello that way to people you're mad at. Is it a test? Oh no, I should apologize quickly. "Sorry," I said finally. "I've been saying that a lot today."

"Hard day? Glad to see you're keeping it together."

"Umm…yeah! Really hard day," I said, scratching the back of my head and looking away.

I knew we weren't supposed to act like we were afraid of them because some of them found it insulting, but that was a tall order.

They wore armor that gleamed in the sun, with large rifles slung over their shoulder, a shorter sidearm on their hips. The armor made them look much larger than they were. One of the soldiers had told Mother about it one day when she was ogling his suit. It's filled with water, which some kind of portable power keeps cool. It's also harder than steel and a hundred times lighter. They wore helmets sometimes that I wasn't sure how they saw through. Some kind of equally advanced technology, I'm sure.

"I'll be going now. I'm sorry." I turned quickly to walk away, to take another route home.

He grabbed me by the arm as I turned, and my stomach felt like it would twist into a dozen knots all at once. I'd never been grabbed by one of them before. Usually, I managed to avoid them altogether.

"You'll need to come with me," he said.

5

He led me by the arm, more like dragged me, for several minutes without a word.

"Hey," I said. "Do you know you're hurting my arm?"

He let go abruptly and turned to me. "Oh…right. The suit. Sorry, it enhances my strength. This is the first time I've worn one. Oh, I'm not supposed to apologize to citizens." He shook his head as if reprimanding himself inside his mind. "I'm Linus, by the way." He made a fist and sighed. "Not supposed to do that either. Mind if we just forget this whole exchange?"

I couldn't help but laugh. "Taylor."

"Nah, soldier, actually. Oh…you meant…wow, I'm really bad at this." He looked away, scratching the back of his head, his cheeks flush. Was he actually embarrassed?

I laughed again, resenting myself a bit for doing so. It must've been his first day. I'm sure after a few more, he'll be just as cruel and rude as most of the others once he'd received better training.

"Taylor. Nice meeting you. I was told to find any stragglers and lead them to the front of the village. Commander wants to give everyone a speech. No idea why, but it seemed important."

I nodded, hoping he'd trip over himself again and offer more bits of information, but he'd composed himself.

"Follow me, please," he said. Pausing for a moment, he corrected himself. "Follow me."

I obeyed. As much as this soldier seemed different from the others, I had to be on my guard. I found him almost hard not to like, but maybe that was a trick. Maybe acting nice to me and then taking me behind an unoccupied house and punching my face was some sick strategy to enhance my adversity. No, Father hated them for a good reason. I was right to, as well. I needed to keep on doing it.

We finally made it back to the front of the village, where he left me in the gathered crowd and took his place behind the commander.

"Just one?" she asked, looking at Linus as he approached.

"One, ma'am," he answered, his tone curt while still being professional. Clearly he hadn't forgotten the proper way to speak to his commander.

She placed her hands behind her, one hand gripping her wrist, resting on the small of her back. Her back was straight, and her head was slightly leaning back. She had red hair, freckled cheeks, and bright green eyes that were similar to Father's. Her suit fit her body shape, except larger. I always found it looked funny on women. All slender and shapely, with a tinier head sticking out of the top. Come to think of it, it looked funny on the men too, to a lesser extent.

Another soldier returned, empty-handed, nodding to his commander before taking his place behind her. This happened a few more times over the next few minutes, with most of the soldiers returning empty-handed, except for one leading two people behind him, one of which was the elderly lady I'd ran into earlier. It irked me that she was being handled so roughly. He had paler skin than Linus, and freckles covered his face. The lady slowed for a moment, and he shoved her, making her stumble forward, nearly falling.

"Move it!" he shouted.

I took a step toward him, but Linus grabbed my arm, pulling me back. I looked up at him, intent on arguing. He offered only a subtle shake of his head as a warning, but the disgust on his face gave away his personal feelings on the matter. Before I could open my mouth, the commander spoke.

"Everyone. Listen carefully to the words I have for you, a gift far kinder than you can imagine, given the circumstances. Indeed, I am putting my own safety at risk by giving you these words." The beautiful flame-haired tyrant droned on, and I mustered up every ounce of will I had to keep from slamming my palm into my forehead if her *kindness* didn't kill me first.

"We have always been kind to all of you, and the adversity we deliver to your young ones is from a place of love and hope for a better future, not just for your people, but for all people." She paced back and forth in front of the crowd, gesturing with her hands as she spoke. It was clear that she was going for the gentle motherly approach, but something in this woman's face gave away her hardness. There was a darkness in her features that I couldn't put into clear thoughts. Almost as though she was eager to get to the next part. The bad part. The threat, and probably a violent one.

"So you can imagine my disappointment," she continued, her tone hardening, "to learn that there are some among you that fail to appreciate our kindness and our dedication to building the character of our next generation.

You must be wondering now why I'm standing before you talking about this when it would be so easy for us to remove this cancer with surgical precision."

She smiled, a poor attempt to once again appear kind. "This is the gift I alluded to. We have decided to allow you to deal with this problem yourselves rather than intervene. We've decided to allow your village to retain as much independence as possible, so long as you continue to earn it. Of course, I'm not permitted to speak of the other adversity zones, but let me assure you that some of them do not enjoy nearly the autonomy that your village does. You see, like the cancer I mentioned, it will spread if not cut out early. So the more it spreads, the grander the action required from us to halt it. Against the judgment of our experts, we will give you one opportunity to deal with the offenders. In the meantime, we will station outside the village and monitor the situation. Your chieftain will communicate with us regularly. We've communicated with him in advance, so he is prepared."

How had they managed to do this, I wondered. Spies? Informants? A long-range communication device? Yes, probably that one. After all, I'd seen the soldiers communicate this way before, touching their ears and speaking to no one there to hear them. Actually, it was probably all three. Our blubbering idiot of a chieftain in action, doing what he probably does best. Why should I be surprised?

Linus shot a glance at me but was quick to look away when our eyes met. Was there something he wanted to tell me? Didn't matter. Not like he'd have the chance to say it, even if he wanted to. More likely, he was toying with me in some cruel way. Send the handsome warrior to fetch the seventeen-year-old, nearly eighteen-year-old girl with rebellious thoughts. Paranoid? Maybe, but I wouldn't put it past them.

"And now, I'll step aside for your chieftain," she said finally.

Gods, no. I'd almost rather they unsling their rifles and start shooting.

He revealed himself from inside the crowd and stepped forward. "I have only a few things to say-uh."

Thank goodness.

He cleared his throat with the gurgling, slimy sound that was unique to him. "I only want to assure our guests that this matter will be resolved with diligence-uh, to show the appreciation that the overwhelming majority of us have for their kindness over the years-uh. We will try peace first, but failing that, we will step aside, and our guests will step in and deal with the traitors. That's all-uh."

He nodded to the commander, who motioned for the rest of her soldiers to follow her. I caught Linus glancing at me again, his expression grim. What was on his mind? I felt my cheeks grow warmer. Maybe I was on his mind. Come on, Taylor, pull yourself together. Now's not the time to have fantasies about handsome warriors coming to sweep you off your feet. Stupid. Grr.

He was trying to tell me something, though. I was almost sure of it. What was it?

They departed, and the rest of us were left to stand around, looking at one another in confusion. Some gullible villagers were no doubt sniffing about for the guilty party, hoping to sell out their own people to win favor from PanTech that would never come. Ever. I didn't want to be the first to leave, but as soon as the crowd started to move, I eagerly moved with it, making my way to my house, hoping no one else would speak to me along the way. Thankfully, no one did.

I stepped through the front door. Father and Mother were already sitting at the table talking. They stopped when they saw me.

"Catch the big speech?" I said, trying to sound apathetic.

"We didn't have a choice," my father grumbled. "They came and knocked on the door and didn't exactly ask."

"At least they knocked," my mother chimed in. "They don't have to, you know. They could have smashed the door down and dragged us out."

"Let them try it. I'd love to—"

The floor started rumbling and furniture shook. At first, just the empty chairs, but soon everything was shaking. A moment later, it stopped, and then a scream. Outside, somewhere. Had they found the rebels?

"Taylor, stay in—"

I bolted out of the door before Mother could finish her sentence.

I looked around, but couldn't spot anything out of the ordinary, and then the scream came again.

"Someone help me!" A woman's voice shrieked again, and a commotion followed. I ran toward it, my head spinning, both from nausea and excitement. The closer I got, the tighter the crowd was, but I forced my way through. I knew this woman! I came to see her animals every week to take care of them. She lived on the edge of the village and owned several pigs. She was crouched over a pig on the ground, breathing heavily and bleeding from some kind of large gash. There had been complaints about her pigs before due to the smell and noise. Had someone taken advantage of the commotion today to kill this one?

"Taylor, thank goodness. Help!"

I ran over as fast as I could, dropping to my knees. "Towel! Rags, something! We have to stop the bleeding."

A man stepped over and yanked off his shirt, tossing it to me. I looked at the wound briefly before covering it. What in the world? It was enormous and looked deep. He wasn't going to survive this....

"I'll do what I can," I lied, trying to comfort her. "What did this to him?"

She sobbed into her apron. "I don't know. I heard him squealing, and I ran out. It was right after the ground shook."

"Did anyone see what happened?" I scanned the crowd, looking at everyone. At first, no one would answer. Finally, a small boy who looked no older than five stepped forward.

"I...I did," he said nervously.

I continued holding the shirt over the pig's wound, but he'd gone still. Nothing could survive a wound that large.

I nodded to the boy before returning my attention to the woman. "I'm sorry. He's gone."

She took a deep breath and sighed, rubbing her face with her sleeve. "You did what you could, dear." She looked to the boy, expectantly, as did I.

"What was it? What did you see?" I asked.

He shook his head. "You won't believe me," he said.

I put my hand on his shoulder. "It's alright. Please, tell us."

He took a deep breath and looked as though he was going to cry. "It was a monster."

6

I kept my hand on his shoulder and held my expression like stone. Several others crowded around couldn't help themselves but cackle in laughter. Others probably wanted to but chose not to out of consideration for the poor woman who'd lost a valuable member of her livestock. Me? I felt sick, sicker than I already was—what a day. My sickness came from deeper down. It was a dread that told me I'd already expected him to say something like that. I knew and didn't want to believe it. It would take a spear larger than any man could carry to make that wound.

"A monster?" I asked, my tone as even as I could make it. "What kind of monster?"

"A giant snake." He choked on his words as if fighting the tears that had become too much for the small child to bear.

"A giant snake…" I said. I'd meant it as a question, but it had come out as a statement. "From the ground? It came from a hole, didn't it?"

"You saw it too?" he asked, his tears temporarily halted by the hope that at least one other person in the village had seen what he'd seen.

"No. Will you please take me to the hole? Can you?" I asked, speaking quietly now.

He nodded.

I turned to the lady. "Please have your pig transported to my clinic. If you do, I'll pay you a fair market price for him.

I want to study that wound more. The sooner, the better, please."

"You really think…" she trailed off.

"The sooner, the better," I repeated before turning my attention back to the boy. "Lead on."

We didn't have to go far; just around the corner of the woman's home was an overturned cart, filled with various tools, all spilled onto the ground. Behind it, there was an enormous hole, sand piled high around it. The hole had to be as wide as my arms outstretched, fingertips to fingertips. If this was what I thought it was, it would be a thing of nightmares, and this would be just the beginning. You'd venture into your nightmares to escape it if you had the choice.

"Brown, like the sand. Speckled gray. Fangs stick out of its mouth, wide in the front but narrow in the back. A head much thicker than the body."

"You did see it!" He hugged my leg.

Oh, how I dreaded that reaction. Gods. A giant Desert Burrower. They made this thing and transported it here. They let it go outside the village, and it was already applying its skill. A skill I'd seen used so many times on small animals outside the gates and sometimes inside. They were fast, had senses like almost nothing else. Maybe the mythical Shadowfalcon topped it, but that was assuming they were real. Father insisted they were, but I assigned mistaken identification to every sighting until I saw one myself. I'd personally seen the Burrower in action. It was one of those experiences that gave you the specific thought that you should let go of a deep breath, relieved that they are one of the smallest snakes and carry no venom due to the unique shape of their fangs. Miniature shovels on both sides, half circle around the front, hollow and open in the back so they can spin under the sand and propel themselves rapidly beneath terrain. The vibration would give it away at least, just before it surfaced, but ironically made it even more terrifying.

"No…but I think I know what it is. Thank you."

I reached into the pouch I'd been carrying in the side pocket of my dress, pulling out the sack of marks the chieftain handed to me earlier. I took one out and gave it to him.

"For me?" he said, his eyebrows furrowed. I didn't blame him. Children learned early to be skeptical of strangers' kindness, seeing that it was so highly frowned upon. If someone from PanTech saw me do this, I'd likely be reprimanded. At this moment, I couldn't care less what PanTech thought. I was more concerned with what they'd done.

"For you," I said and nodded in the affirmative. "Let's keep the payment our little secret. Say you found it in the sand."

He nodded vigorously, his eyes flashing with the useless knickknacks he could use this mark to purchase and, for just a moment, seeming to forget the horrific creature he'd seen.

"Run along, and maybe play inside for the next few days."

He ran but turned briefly to wave at me as he did. It was useless to ask him to keep that to himself. He practically broadcasted his appreciation to the whole world, with just the look on the face and the newfound bounce in his step. It very well could have been the first time anything like that had happened to him. Both things that had happened to him...

I hated PanTech so much. So much that, if there were some way for them to read minds, I'd be setting off every alarm at the moment. I couldn't tell the village to prepare. I couldn't offer my theory on where this creature came from. PanTech would deny it, as they always did with their tricks. They'd pretend to help. I'd have requested the one rifle the village was allowed to use, that every villager is allowed to fire ten times on his or her sixteenth birthday. Enough to become familiar with the function of the weapon. The trigger, the sights, the recoil, the noise. But not enough to become proficient. I had a knack for it, though. Enough that after the fifth and sixth round high bullseye, that I intentionally missed the last four shots almost completely.

Besides, I needed the authorization of a PanTech soldier to take it out on loan.

Wait...

Linus! What if he did have an eye for me? I could use that. I certainly couldn't threaten him or beat up another soldier and take their rifle. I wouldn't know how to use it anyway. It looked almost completely different from the old wood, metal, and smoke relic that exploded projectiles from brass-cased rounds and held ten magazine shots. I felt gross at the thought. What if Linus really was a nice man, and I took advantage of his feelings? What if I got him punished or even killed?

No...this was PanTech. I couldn't allow for such soft emotions. The sick feeling reminded me of the pig and put me back in the moment. I needed to have a look at it. Hopefully, they had it over at the clinic already. This snake shouldn't have venom, but I didn't put anything past PanTech. If they'd managed to create a giant one, maybe this one had venom or even shoots the venom from its fangs. Perhaps it could see in the dark. Maybe its scales were as hard as steel. I shook my head. Definitely not the thoughts I needed to be having if I wanted to be in the moment.

I jogged back toward the clinic, finding that four men had just dropped the pig onto one of my wooden examination tables under an open canopy. My first thought was that I hadn't cleaned it yet before I realized it didn't matter. I thanked them and began my examination. It was too bad I'd given Cara the day off today. I really could have used her help to take notes. It would all have to be in my head today. After another moment of consideration, I decided that was indeed for the best. A written record of my findings probably wouldn't be great for my health or the health of those around me.

I unlocked a box behind me and pulled out a long wooden rod. I inserted it into the wound, pushing it gently as far as I could, marking the depth with my fingers, and making a mental note of the length. Large enough to have easily swallowed the pig and dragged him down his tunnel. Easily. So, why didn't it?

Assuming they are like the normal burrower, they rarely fail to retrieve the prey they've bitten, unless they're young and inexperienced. Oh no…What if it's a baby? It would grow enormous. Even all of the animals outside the village couldn't sustain it. It would hunt us too, and we'd be easier targets. It would wipe us out before it became fully grown.

I took a deep breath and composed myself. Inexperienced. That was the critical part. If PanTech brought it here, it was probably grown and cared for in some kind of special environment. A big expensive lab, where they'd feed it on a cycle, and it would never have to hunt. It's new to hunting. That's why it bit the pig but didn't pull it back through the tunnel. Maybe the kid spooked it, but as soon as it realizes that we're no more dangerous than the pig, that won't last long. It's possible that if it came from PanTech, it would be somewhat tame to humans…unless they took precautions against that somehow. In either scenario, this meant that we need to kill the snake quickly. The more time it took, the more it would adapt to the environment around it. The more experienced it would be with hunting, and if it kills a human, it'll come back. None of its other prey will be as tightly packed as we are. This was a disaster….

I rubbed my forehead with my forearm. Right, I didn't even look for venom on the rod. There was no guarantee I'd see it, especially if it was unique to this animal and something I'd never seen before. I examined the tissue around the wound. There were no signs along the edge of venom that often spilled from the initial wound. Pig's tongue was normal, and eyes appeared normal. I breathed a sigh of relief. It seemed to be a mostly identical version of the normal burrower, but I wondered what difference that really made. The wound was too deep to even tell how deep it was. All I could tell was that it was huge but not quite huge enough to go through the other side. Even that wasn't a certainty because it could have failed to get a complete bite. Still, the estimate I could make seemed consistent with the size of the hole it burrowed.

We could plug the holes we find with poison and hope that it came back through and accidentally ingests it. Cross our fingers that would do the trick. Not likely. They rarely use the same holes twice unless they come back immediately to chase wounded prey. Once they retreat, the burrowed tunnel collapses quickly beneath the unstable sand.

I couldn't tell Mother and Father. If I got caught, they'd be implicated, assuming they don't end up being implicated anyway. At least if they genuinely didn't know what I'd intended, maybe they'd let them off. Ferris couldn't join me, even if he wanted to. He was going to be useless for at least a week, or more. If I went and simply asked the chieftain for the rifle, he'd report me for doing it unauthorized. I was fairly certain he knew already. Who could help me?

I stood there, racking my brain for a long while, and finally accepted the reality. No one. No one could help me. Even if I could manipulate Linus into authorizing my use of the rifle for some other reason, I had to hunt and kill this monster on my own…somehow. Fantastic.

7

I considered what I might do with the pig's carcass or if there was anything I really could do with it. I entertained the thought of using it for bait but remembered that wasn't how Burrowers hunted. They felt the vibrations on the sand, ripped out of their tunnel, and stole their prey away. The pig wouldn't do much good for that. There was always eating the pig. After all, I would be paying for it, but I didn't want to risk that PanTech may have found a way to make the venom undetectable through normal means. In the end, the very inconvenient course of action I found to be best was to roll the thing out of the village and dump it far away so the carrion and scavengers that roamed the desert would eat it. Vultures would make short work of it.

Once I'd done that, the daylight was spent, and so was I. The snake needed dealing with, but there was nothing I could do about it for now, and I certainly couldn't tell anyone what I was planning. My father was waiting for me when I came through the door. A candle was burning on the table in front of him, and he was reading a book.

"Did you find out what caused that quake earlier?" he said, not looking up from his book.

So much for sneaking to my room without him talking to me. I should've known that would never happen. I considered for a moment what kind of lie I would tell. Should I lie? If I told him the truth, what would happen? Lying to Father felt about as wrong as wrong can be, and in the end, I couldn't do it. Not entirely, at least. A half-truth would have to do—a compromise to ease my conscience.

"A snake bit a pig, actually."

"And…that caused a quake?" he looked up at me as I sat at the table across from him, tilting his head.

I shrugged my shoulders. "Seems so."

He chuckled, and sat the book on the table, face-down, leaning back more comfortably in his chair. "Please."

"Please, what?" I asked.

"Please explain that to me. I'm not sure I understand how a snake biting a pig causes a quake. Must've been a pretty big snake or pig."

"How's Ferris?" I asked, trying my odds at changing the subject.

He sighed, narrowing his eyes at me. His eyes said *I want you to know that I know what you're doing, but I can see you're exhausted so, I'll play along.*

"Your brother has been in much pain. You can see it on his face, but he won't admit it, of course. The wound has worsened, as terror ant bites tend to do. It will likely worsen more over the next few days before it begins to heal." He paused, as if he'd just remembered something else. "Please don't blame yourself for it, Tay."

I shook my head. "Right. You were in the room when I had that nightmare. It's…I'm alright. I'm just glad he made it out with just the one bite, as terrible as one bite is. The ants were devouring him in my dream, but that could have easily been real. In the dream, he blamed me, but I know he wouldn't really. He…I bet he put you up to talk to me about it, am I right?"

He smiled and nodded once.

"I knew it. Brave in all the wrong ways."

I wished I could take the words back the moment they left my lips. Partly because it was unfair to my brother, and partly because Father was going to ask me.

"Why do you say that?" he asked, in perfect sync with my thoughts.

"I don't know. I guess I just hate to see him so brainwashed by PanTech. Everyone worships them like they're some kind of savior doing us a favor. They make our life better by making our lives worse? How messed up is that?"

"You'll get no argument from me about PanTech, but as frustrated as I get with the people of the village for not seeing them for who they are, they are both the oppressor and the savior for anyone looking to move from citizen to employee. Your own test will be coming up soon. Your brother will be testing with you, since he was barely too young for the last one. Or, have you chosen to stay in the village?"

In truth, while I hadn't really thought about it, I couldn't see myself leaving the village. Sure, Cara could take over as the vet. After all, she has almost as much training as me, but I just didn't feel ambitious, and I certainly did *not* want to help PanTech.

"They say that they have a veterinary laboratory beyond our comprehension. Imagine what you could study there if you were assigned to that section."

I grinned. "So, why didn't you go? Didn't you have one of the highest test scores ever recorded from this village?"

"Haven't I told you before? I get your point. I wanted to stay in the village so I could continue developing some of my inventions here. I wanted to make everyone's life here better. It was foolish of me not to expect what came next. Of course, as soon as I'd given up my chance at a high-level position at their technology institute, they sent soldiers here to destroy my inventions, and they forbade me from recreating them, further developing them, or creating new ones. They told me that it interfered with the adversity experienced by young villagers. They gave me a choice, you know, before they destroyed them. I could continue working on the inventions, but they'd have to offset their benefit with more artificially-imposed challenges to the village. More confiscated food. Introduction of new illnesses. Modifying native animal species to make them more dangerous."

I blurted out before I could stop myself. "Wait, they've done that before?"

Of course, Father picked up on the meaning behind what I'd said immediately. "Before? You mean…they've done it again? Tay, is that what you meant by the snake biting a pig caused the quake?"

Stupid. Stupid Taylor. I'd gotten him entirely off the topic. He wasn't even thinking about that anymore, then I go and sabotage myself.

"I'm not sure."

"I don't know, that sounded sure to me. They've somehow created a snake that's able to cause quakes? Why didn't I hear about such a thing passing through the village?"

I rubbed my forehead. I must've been close to collapsing from exhaustion. Today must've been the longest day of my life to this point.

"That's because it didn't pass through the village," I said. "It burrowed beneath, emerged, bit the pig, and escaped through its tunnel."

"A burrower, then. But that doesn't explain the quake. How do you know the snake was responsible?"

I stared at him blankly for a moment. I was quickly losing the energy to explain anything, and I knew it would come to him.

"Oh no...really?"

I nodded. "Yes."

"It's that big?"

"Enormous," I confirmed.

"Because of the rebels they've discovered...."

"That was my suspicion, too. Keep this between us, please. I don't want the whole town panicking, and they'll target us when they realize it came from me."

"You examined the pig, didn't you?" he asked.

I nodded. "I've been considering how I might deal with it, but I need more time to come up with something. I think tomorrow I'll visit the PanTech camp outside the village."

He furrowed his brow but said nothing.

"I'm going to go see a boy there. I think he's just a little older than me. Actually, I think he likes me. We ran into each other in town before the big speech, and he introduced himself to me. Pretty unusual for a soldier."

"Please be careful, Tay. I'm not sure it's a good idea to approach them directly like that."

"He's pretty handsome, too," I added.

"Tay...," his tone darkened, and the hint of sadness in his voice gave me a twinge of guilt. I'd only meant to tease him.

"I mean it. He wasn't like the other soldiers. Maybe he could tell me something about it. I don't think he'd hurt me if that's what you're worried about."

"Never trust PanTech," he said.

"I trust my instincts. They're all I have."

He pondered this for a moment before grunting slightly and nodding.

"Good night."

I stood up and stepped around the table, hugging him tightly around the neck.

"Good night," he said, not looking up at me again, already falling deep into his own thoughts. Maybe he was also considering ways to deal with the monster, but I'd get to it first. I didn't tell him that the real reason I was going to see Linus was to convince him to authorize my loan of the rifle and some ammunition. He'd have probably tried to lock me in my room if I'd told him that.

Thinking of my room, I wasn't sure I'd ever been so happy to see it when I finally went through its door. The bed, most of all. I frowned when I noticed the pile of broken glass still sitting on the table next to my bed, yet another reminder of how terrible this day had been. I picked up the largest piece and took a few moments to study my appearance. I wished that I looked more like my father instead of my mother. My reflection was almost like looking into her eyes, only with darker skin. She would always say that made me even more beautiful than her. Mother, of course, was not one for modesty. Then again, perhaps it was Mother I should seek advice from before seeing Linus tomorrow. I'm sure she'd have a lot to say about how I could manipulate boys into doing whatever I wanted. She'd say I was an exotic beauty to him, and I should wear my finest cultural dress.

Just the thought made me angry, no matter how right she was. I wanted to study and make new discoveries like Father had when he was young, not have some man take care of me while I experimented with scented oils and skin moisturizers.

I laid out my work clothing, almost to spite her in my mind. Maybe Linus would appreciate a woman who could perform a pig autopsy in the desert heat or bury her arm elbow-deep in a camel. Perhaps he'd appreciate my mind more than my body. Maybe....

What was I thinking? All I needed to do was to get him to agree to authorize my use of the rifle. I didn't need him to ask me to marry him. *Come on, Taylor. Pull it together.*

I collapsed onto my bed, burying my face into the pillow. I wanted to scream into it, but I was afraid someone would somehow hear me. It didn't matter anyway because I was asleep before I could even finish the thought.

8

As I dreamed, I found myself again lying on the hot desert sand. My muscles loose and relaxed. The sun was wrapping me in a reassuring glow. A gentle breeze softened the heat enough to shift it from uncomfortable to comforting. My eyes were closed, allowing only a soft light into my vision.

I felt a hand gently touch my shoulder, but I wasn't startled. I opened my eyes and realized it was Linus, dressed in our cultural clothing. He was smiling at me, and his blue eyes felt so real, matching the sky so well that it was as though they were transparent as he leaned above me. I smiled back, and he leaned down slowly and met my lips with a soft kiss. I wrapped my arms around his neck, pulling him closer, meeting his kiss more deeply.

As I kissed him, he was yanked from my arms with a scream. I saw him being pulled away from me, toward the sky, and as he was pulled further away, I saw the snake that had appeared behind him. It pierced his body with its enormous fangs, pouring blood onto the desert floor. He punched and kicked at the snake's head with futility. As he hung from its jaws, it looked at me, silent and still, hovering above me like a serpent god, demonstrating his power.

Finally, Linus stopped struggling, and I knew that he'd died. His body became limp, his limbs dangling, his head wobbling slightly in the breeze as the snake continued to threaten me with his stare. He seemed to carry neither good nor evil intent with it—just a god indulging his hunger with insignificant beings.

Linus turned his head slowly toward me, his gentle smile returning, but with tears falling from his eyes onto the sand below.

"You did this," he whispered.

No. No, no, no, no, I sobbed, shouting the words in my mind, but I couldn't speak.

"You did this," he said again, his voice rising to a shout this time.

I filled with rage. I wanted to leap to my feet and tear off the snake's head with my bare hands. I wanted to smash him with the sun itself. I wanted to rip his fangs from his jaws and gouge out his eyes with them. My sadness gave way to a fury I rarely allowed myself to feel, a fury that threatened to swallow me whole.

And then, I was awake, sitting up in my bed so quickly it's a wonder I hadn't toppled onto the floor. My skin was wet with cold sweat, and I breathed as though I'd been running for hours. What did that dream mean? Did it mean anything?

A feeling of guilt suddenly gripped me. What if Linus was really as kind as he seemed? What if he did like me? What if he's not like most of the other soldiers, and I get him in trouble, or worse?

I rubbed the small tears away from my eyes. What a pointless thing to worry about. What was I supposed to do, let the snake kill everyone in the whole village? What if it was my father who was snatched by it next, or my brother, or mother, or Cara, or the kind old lady I met yesterday? Even if he was the kindest PanTech soldier ever to live, this is something I had to do. Sacrifices had to be made, even if what I had to sacrifice was a part of myself.

I rubbed my eyes again and stood up, getting dressed in my tattered work clothing, not unlike what all the village men and women wore when planning a day of labor. As I reached the door, I thought of Mother and sat back onto my bed, reaching into the drawer of the table beside my bed, pulling out the comb she'd given me. I spent the next several minutes combing my hair before tying it into a loose ponytail.

After I left my room, I stepped into the common area, hoping to avoid a conversation. Luckily, aside from Mother, I was the first one up. Her back was to me, cooking. I did my best to sneak quietly to the door, but, as expected, she heard me and turned around before I could reach it.

"Good morning. My, your hair is beautiful."

I inhaled deeply, putting on a smile that was somewhere between false and genuine. "Thank you. I finally took your advice, I suppose."

She looked down at my clothes, and I waited for her to criticize them, but she didn't. Her smile never weakened.

"I'm sure Father told you, but I'm going to head out to the camp today and see a boy named Linus I met yesterday. I may not be back until later, so don't worry about lunch." I reached for the door, resting my hand on the handle before she stopped me again.

"Yes, your father told me. I can only assume that you're going to see him because there's something you need from him."

"It's not like…," I started to protest, but wasn't it true?

"Sorry, dear, I didn't mean to make that sound like an insult. It wasn't. It was only an observation. I know you haven't had any interest in boys. I also know you don't particularly enjoy hearing my advice, but I would suggest you start considering it. It is a hard world, and there is a reason some women would kill to have your naturally beautiful appearance. You could see it as an insult to them to take it for granted, as though you weren't fortunate."

I sighed, clenching my teeth. "Mother…."

She chuckled, which surprised me. "Maybe work on your charm a bit, though. That's a skill that can be learned, regardless of your fortune at birth. Here, I made something for you." She pulled two small sacks from the counter and held them out for me.

I eyed them suspiciously, my anxiety building for what sort of contents these bags may have in them. "What are those?"

"Your lunch," she said. Then she added a wink. "And his. Salt-cured ham and bread I baked early this morning. Oh, and this." She reached behind her and fetched a bottle, handing it to me.

"Is that…cactus wine?" I asked.

"For you, only a few sips. For him, as much as he'll drink as long as he behaves."

My cheeks had already started burning. Should I thank my mother? Be furious with her? I wasn't sure anymore, but if it got me that rifle….

I grasped the bottle of wine.

"Small cups are in the sacks. Be careful, and remember that it's better to make someone your pawn than to become one." She reached out and moved a wisp of hair aside that had drifted onto my face.

"Thank you," I finally decided to say. "Really. Thanks."

She smiled, reaching down and opening the door for me, gently squeezing my arm.

Well, that was awkward, but Mother's coming-of-age conversations that had become more frequent in the last year were always awkward. I wasn't sure if that was her or me. Considering how enchanted everyone had always been with Mother, including my father, I could only assume it was me. *Guest*, I reminded myself. Not *soldier*. Not *invader*. Not *oppressor*. Not *enemy*. I couldn't let my words betray my thoughts.

I stopped by the clinic and gave Cara what she would no doubt find to be bad news.

She was only a year younger than me but petite. One might've guessed she was fourteen by looking at her and would've felt even more confident when they heard her small voice that matched her appearance perfectly.

"Hey there. It's going to be a busy day, with us being closed yesterday. You excited?" she asked, her fist pump making me believe there was no sarcasm in the question.

"Ah, uh, well…," I started.

She jutted out her bottom lip and crossed her arms. "Oh no, please don't tell me you're going out again today."

I scratched the back of my head. "I'm sorry, Cara. I really owe you one."

She slapped her cheeks and pulled her hands down her face, stretching her eyes and mouth toward her chest. "Ugh!" she groaned. "I'll do my best."

"I know you will," I said, smiling. I did know. Cara was one of the most reliable people in the village, and we'd become good friends since we started working together at the clinic. Even though I barely had more training than her, she never once complained about being my assistant. In fact, I think she was relieved. She might've run screaming if the clinic was suddenly handed over to her. "Good luck," she added.

"You too. Thanks."

I made my way to the gate, then through it into the desert before realizing I had no idea where this camp would be set up. What if I'd misunderstood, and they'd set up camp beyond the barrier? No, if the chieftain was sending messengers, they'd have to be inside the barrier, but that still could be anywhere within a several-mile radius of the village.

I stopped and looked around. It made sense that they wouldn't circle halfway around the village before going off to their camp. Odds were it was a straight shot from the gate if I was careful.

So, following that logic, I walked for several minutes in the straightest line I could manage. After a while, I found myself just short of the barrier, stopping next to one of the markers staked deeply into the sand. I looked around in all directions but didn't see anything at all. No smoke was rising. No raucous yelling. No visible tracks from their vehicles. I sat down in the sand, looking down at my feet.

Way to go, Taylor. Step one of your big plan is such a great success. It's surely a great omen of what's to come. I was...embarrassed, to put it lightly, so I wasn't about to show my face to Cara or my mother again so soon. Where could they be? Is it possible they lied about being nearby to intimidate the rebels into behaving? A bluff? I placed my hands on top of my head, racking my brain.

After an hour of this, I'd finally accepted defeat. Maybe if I got back early enough, I could think of a way to pry the information from the chieftain. Maybe I could tell him I had information about the rebels and wanted to go personally?

No. It could work, but more than likely, he'd insist on sending his own messengers, or he'd demand I tell him first and then…what? I'd have to make something up or be punished myself. Going to see the chieftain was riskier than just walking into the PanTech camp. Maybe I could just ask around and see if any of the villagers saw them while out hunting or saw what direction they went in when they left. Maybe, maybe, maybe. I could really go for a "definitely" right now.

I only made it about ten steps back in the direction of the village when a gust of wind came bearing a gift. Now, that was an odd smell. A good smell. A PanTech breakfast, no doubt, or what was left of it. I turned and traveled in the direction it came from and did not make it far before a tent came into sight. As I got even closer, I could hear talking.

When I got within shouting distance, I heard a chirping sound, and the talking ceased. A moment later, five soldiers were stepping out of the camp to meet me. Each one had their rifle pointed at me, their expressions unreadable at this distance, but I'm sure well within range to kill me.

"Umm…," I said, before clearing my throat, and raising my voice to a shout to be sure they heard me. "Our welcome guests," I continued. "I'm here to see Linus if that's alright." I offered the biggest, friendliest smile a seventeen-year-old girl could offer with five rifles aimed at her head.

9

The five soldiers kept their rifles pointed directly at me, saying nothing and making no movement, indicating that they'd heard me in the first place.

I took a deep breath. "Hello! I'd like to see Linus, please!" I shouted much louder than the last time. Surely they'd heard me the first time.

After a few moments longer, one lowered his rifle and looked to the others. "Wow, did she say 'Linus'?"

Another shrugged. "Leave it to that idiot to tell the first pretty face he sees where the camp's located."

A third soldier spoke. "It's not like it's hidden. We've had two citizens stumble in here by accident already. It's not like we're on a management mission." He was promptly elbowed. I suppose I wasn't supposed to hear about management missions. It wasn't as if I knew what they were, but I could venture a few guesses.

The first to lower his rifle looked up at me. "Stay right there. One more step, and we'll shoot. Understand?"

I clenched my teeth. What was I supposed to do? Run in there and knife everyone before they could turn me into a red mist with their rifles? "Yeah, okay. I'll just…sit here." I sat on the sand. Maybe that would be less threatening.

After a moment, another soldier walked up to them, looked out to me, and removed his helmet. Thankfully, it was Linus, hopefully here to tell them I wasn't a threat to five armed PanTech super soldiers. He squinted and held his hand above his brow to shield his eyes from the sun.

"Taylor? Is that you?"

"You remembered me!" I shouted, pretending to be surprised, except part of me genuinely was surprised.

"You remembered *me*!" His smile reached his eyes. He stepped forward, then turned back to the other soldiers. "Tell the commander I'm taking some of my downtime outside the camp."

I wished they didn't have those helmets on. It was impossible to read their expressions or even be sure they were human. Sometimes I wondered anyway, with or without the helmet.

The soldiers didn't answer. Just turned and walked back into the camp as Linus strolled out to meet me, holding his helmet to his side, his rifle slung across his back.

"I was just starting to get used to the idea that I'd probably never see you again, but I'm glad I was wrong. I haven't been able to get you out of my mind since I saw you yesterday," he said, far more candidly than I expected. Just as I felt my cheeks flush with heat, it was countered by a low ache in my heart.

Please don't be the man you seem to be, said my heart, at the thought of hurting him if it were true. *But, that would be ideal for the plan*, said my brain, ever so slightly louder.

"I've…thought about you a lot too. I…um…." *Come on, Taylor.* "Will you have lunch with me? It would've been breakfast, but I got a little lost."

"Sure. I'd love to. Truth be told, until I'm called for a mission, I've got all kinds of time. I save it up and cash it out, usually because I don't get along so well with the other soldiers." He stopped a moment, looking away and scratching his chin. "Sorry, wrong way to say it. I get along with them fine. We're just not good friends. We don't spend time together off the clock. I mean…," his face began to turn red. "I'm talking too much," he finally said, with a big sigh.

I giggled involuntarily. I hated that I seemed to do that with him before I could realize it and stop myself. "It's alright. I probably know less about your world than you do about mine, so I enjoy hearing it, really. But, let's talk over lunch. There's a couple of big rocks a little ways from here that make some shade this time of day. Hope you like salt-cured ham."

He didn't answer. Not with words anyway. His smile said enough as it got just a little bit brighter.

We walked away from the camp and finally arrived at the rocks. I spread out a blanket on the sand and sat, pulling items out of the sacks my mother had given me.

"Wow, you made all of this?"

"I wish," I said with a weak laugh. "My mother made these."

Should have lied, Taylor.

His expression darkened. "That's one of those things a lot of people miss when they leave. You'll never see or hear from your parents again. My old man wasn't a good man. Got killed when I was just a boy over a game of cards. My mom was the only person I ever met that was meaner than *he* was. She was pretty sick when I left. Guessing she's dead by now."

I stared at him blankly for a moment, trying to think of something comforting to say, but all I could manage to do was frown awkwardly for an uncomfortably long time.

"I…sorry to hear that. I'm guessing that made you a good candidate for PanTech though, with all your troubles?"

Wow. Couldn't have said something more stupid than that if you tried.

He laughed at that. "Sure, I suppose. I was pretty good with guns too. Joined up with a posse and caused a lot of trouble. Mostly robbed. Got into the occasional gunfight. Earned myself the nickname 'Blue-Eyed Devil' after one real nasty incident."

Strange. The more he talked about this, the more his speaking and accent seemed to change.

"Your voice," I said. "You sound a little different."

He scratched the back of his head. "Oh, right. Sorry. Seems that's one of my bigger problems. Despite being a pretty smart guy, I never seem to learn. When you arrive, they work to assimilate you into PanTech culture. You'll learn how you should be dressing, and speaking, how to hide your accent, and things like that."

With a smile, I handed him a slice of ham and bread. I was starting to understand why he found himself at odds with authority. "I bet you haven't tried cactus wine before."

He grinned. "You'd be right. Pour the cup full, if you don't mind. We're not allowed to have alcohol in the camp."

I did as he asked and handed it over to him. He took a big drink, then another, and another until the cup was completely empty. He passed it back to me with an even bigger grin than before.

"Thank you, Taylor. That really hit the spot." He bit into his ham, never taking his eyes off me as he chewed.

We ate silently for a few minutes without speaking, and he finally let his smile rest. Not for long, though.

He grinned, looking me in the eyes. "Let the two of us be frank with one another," he said.

"Umm…about what? You want to hear about my life in the village?" I asked, hoping that's what he meant. It wasn't.

"I think you know what I mean," he said, taking another bite of his ham.

I did know what he meant, but I wasn't about to blow my cover just yet, no matter how poorly thought out and lousy it was.

"Sure. I'm not a big fan of the cactus wine."

He tried not to laugh because his mouth was full now, but he failed, and part of it escaped his mouth before he threw his hand up to his face to stop it.

"What do you do for a living?" he quickly asked, his embarrassment—over losing part of his food in front of me—taking his confident talk down a notch.

"I'm a veterinarian."

He raised his eyebrow and let out a whistle. "You don't say?" He looked around. "Camels, and livestock, I reckon?"

"You what? Reckon?"

He rubbed his chin. "Sorry. I mean to say, do you take care of the livestock around here? This is my first time here, but I saw pigs and camels."

"I do. And pets, of course."

"Pets?" He looked at me as though he didn't believe what I was saying.

"Right, sorry. Some people keep lizards; we have mice out here, and of course, snakes."

He flinched a bit at the mention of snakes, and I didn't miss it.

"What about you? Do you have any pets?"

"No, I don't. I think I want something a little different, but nothing's ever really connected with me. Besides, I see plenty of other people's pets."

He nodded. "I had a horse once, before I left for PanTech. Had a dog when I was younger, but my pop shot him after he bit him. Was a good dog."

He seemed more distant all of a sudden as if the memory was dragging him back in.

"What's a...dog?"

He grinned. "You should try to pass your test and become an employee. You'll discover all kinds of new things. A lot more than dogs, assuming you think that life can be for you."

"Is it for you?" I asked, genuinely curious.

"No. I thought it would be. I thought I'd get there, and everything would be perfect. Finally, no more robbing or shooting people who didn't deserve to be shot, but it's the same thing, just with bigger guns and a bigger gang."

"They'll kill you if they hear you say that," I said coldly.

"Nah, it's not that bad. I've said worse," he admitted. "Now, about this plan of yours?"

Ah, I'd expected him to be duller than this, but it seems I just caught him in an awkward moment yesterday. He still seemed to really like me, though, so maybe....

"I need you to vouch for me to use the village's rifle."

He frowned, then sighed, but returned to his smile almost as quickly, as though he knew the answer before he'd asked.

"What do you need the rifle for? A lady like you shouldn't be doing the kind of dangerous things I'm betting you're about to do. You should let a man handle it."

"I'm *not* a *lady* like apparently where you're from, and I can handle myself fine, thank you!" I threw the contents of my glass of wine into his face and leaned forward, snatching up the blanket and stuffing it back into my pack. "I'll find another way."

I started to turn away, but I felt his hand grab my arm, firmly, but much more gently than yesterday. I whipped around and socked him in the jaw, sending him stumbling back a step, which probably surprised me more than it did him. He released my arm.

"Okay, I get it. I was wrong, and that was a stupid thing to say. Forgive me?" He rubbed his jaw. "Oh, and nice punch. You as good with that rifle as you are with your fist?"

"Better," I said, still feeling a wave of anger. Directed at the wrong person, as usual. I was lucky he didn't slap my head off with his super armor hand. Instead, he was already smiling again. It was almost intoxicating, the way he answered everything with a smile.

"In that case, I'll do it on one condition."

"You want a kiss?"

His face contorted. "What? Uh, no, I mean…do you want to?" He slapped himself in the forehead and pulled his hand slowly down his face. "Sorry, I mean…," he took a deep breath and exhaled, his face turning red. "That was a joke. You made a joke. Sorry."

I smiled. Suddenly, I wanted to tell him it wasn't a joke, in a way I hadn't expected I would, but I had to hide that. For now, at least.

"Just that you seem like a lot of fun, and I'm owed the downtime to do whatever I want with. It beats playing cards with a bunch of boring 'yes sirs' and 'no sirs.' I want to join you to hunt the snake."

"But I never said—" I started, but he cut me off.

"You didn't have to say. I never liked the idea of bringing that thing here in the first place, and I had a feeling that's what this was all about. Don't look at it as help. Look at it as doing me a favor in exchange. An equal trade between gunslingers. Deal?" He held out his hand.

I looked down at it a moment. I must be completely insane. Beyond all hope insane. This is probably the single worst thing I could possibly do, for him, and for me. I was going to regret this, and I knew it. I didn't know when or how much. Only that I would.

"Deal," I said, gripping his hand tightly in a handshake.

10

Linus and I made our way back to town, garnering our share of ogling as we entered the gate. It was rare for a lone PanTech soldier to enter the town, especially walking side-by-side with a citizen, and the other villagers couldn't have made that any more obvious. No one dared to say anything aloud, but I guessed that most didn't approve of our being together. If I had to distill it down even further, it was probably my arrogance of walking next to him. I should be following, head bowed, eyes averted, in complete awe. My mother would have approved of that. At least, I think she would have. It was becoming harder and harder to tell anymore.

Since everyone was afraid to talk to me with my new companion, it wasn't long before we made it to the chieftain's home. I knocked on the door, and waited, and waited, and waited. Eventually he came to the door, and one of the village girls, about my age, ran out as he opened it. She didn't look up at me. Just hurried away like she was escaping a burning house.

The chieftain looked at me, waggled his eyebrows, and laughed. Linus had stood off to the side, looking at some of the items stacked outside the chieftain's house to pass the time, so no one noticed him yet.

I stared at him for a moment, my blood boiling, calling upon the divine power I needed not to put my hands around his throat.

"Well-uh?"

I didn't answer. I couldn't, yet. I was still cooling my rage. It didn't take long for him to become impatient, just watching me glare at him. "Listen here-uh, you stupid girl. How about I knock out some of those pretty teeth of yours-uh? Will that give your tongue more room to talk-uh?"

Linus had already started walking over. He stood in front of me and locked eyes with him.

"Good afternoon, Chieftain. I'm here to authorize the loan of your village's rifle to this girl. One-hundred rounds of ammunition."

Their eyes remained locked.

"Heh…uh…the rule states ten rounds-uh."

Linus grinned, shrugged his shoulders, raised his hands in mock defeat, then turned to look at me. "Sorry, looks like your chieftain is going to try to override me on this one. Maybe he thinks I'm too stupid to count." He turned to look back to the chieftain. "Right? Am I too stupid to count?"

The chieftain didn't answer, sweat beading on his bloated cheeks.

"No? Too stupid to know the rules, then? That must be it. Too stupid to know the rules." He turned back to me, smiling, before offering that smile back to the chieftain, then breaking out into laughter.

The chieftain looked nervously between Linus and me several times before chuckling himself.

Suddenly, Linus grabbed him by the collar of the shirt and flung him back into his house, sending him toppling over a table and knocking over two chairs that had been pushed beneath it.

I was frightened for a moment. I hadn't seen that coming, and it was violence I hadn't yet seen from him. He'd been nothing but gentle and kind with me. For a moment, my stomach twisted at the memory of throwing the wine into his face earlier. I guess he did like me after all. Thank goodness.

The chieftain struggled to his feet, his eyes wide. "My…my…uh…," he swallowed hard. "My apologies. I was only joking."

Linus kept his gaze cold and even, not even a hint of softness in his eyes. "When you come back around the corner, you better make sure that rifle isn't pointing my way, or I'll show you what a real joke looks like. Except I'll be the only one laughing. Now go!"

The chieftain scrambled toward a different part of his home, tripping over one of the chairs he'd knocked over, before returning to his feet and running out of our sight.

Linus looked down at me, smiled, and gave me a thumbs-up. "How'd I do?" he whispered.

My eyes were still wide, and I just slowly shook my head from side-to-side.

"Oh no. Did I overdo it? I overdid it, didn't I? Wow, PanTech really is nicer to you guys than they are to other places. This is how they all acted in my zone."

All I could manage was a weak, "I'm sorry."

He tilted his head, hoping for more of an explanation.

"I'm sorry," I continued, "You shouldn't be, though. He's not a good man. He deserved that and worse."

This seemed to relieve him a bit, but the implication that it was all an act wasn't something I bought. It didn't look rehearsed; it looked practiced. Linus hadn't been exaggerating when he talked about his past. Still, you didn't get far in this world by being soft. I wished that weren't the truth, but it was, and I knew that. I didn't need the help of a poet or musician. I didn't want any help at all, but if it was going to be forced on me, an experienced gunslinger with a mean streak certainly wasn't the worst thing that could be thrown my way. A hypnotically handsome gunslinger with a mean streak, wavy blonde hair, deep blue eyes, and seemed to like me was even better for some reason.

The chieftain came back around the corner, sweat now dripping freely from his chin onto his soaked shirt. He was carrying what I assumed was the rifle, wrapped in cloth, tied tightly with a string in several places, and a lidded metal bucket. He started to hand the rifle to Linus, but Linus instead nodded to me, who he passed it to instead.

"I'm not going to find any problems with this rifle, am I? It's your duty to maintain it, as we taught you."

"No. Of course not. It's well-maintained. This, I promise you."

"Will I find myself short on ammunition?"

He shook his head. "No. No. One-hundred rounds, as you requested."

"Thank you. Oh, and just one more thing." Linus smiled and took a step toward the chieftain, who recoiled reflexively.

"Y-yes?"

"That girl who left here when we arrived. Did you think I didn't notice?"

"Wha...what?"

Linus punched the wall next to the door, burying his fist into it, sending the chieftain cowering with his hands held above his head as if his entire house was about to collapse on him. "You going to imply I'm stupid again? We speak the same language. If you say 'what' one more time, I'll break your fingers."

"Linus!" I grabbed his arm, but he pushed me back, sending me stumbling backward and falling onto the ground. Several villagers had gathered around now, mumbling amongst themselves, no one daring to speak loud enough for Linus or the chieftain to hear them.

"I…uh…I've no doubt you noticed. She's nobody. What do you care about her?"

Linus reached over, grabbed his hand, and with a sickening crack, broke his finger. I put both of my hands over my mouth and gasped. What had I done by agreeing to bring him here? What if he treated everyone this way and was only kind to me because we were still within sight of his colleagues? What if he hurt more people?

"I heard a 'what.'" Linus still held his hand, the chieftain on his knees now, gasping in pain. "I saw her face when she ran out. If you bring any of the village girls in here again, I'm going to be back, and next time, I'll make sure there are no ladies present to remind me of my manners. Do you understand?"

The chieftain looked at him, his cheeks vibrating as he shook but turned his head away.

Linus moved to the next finger, slowly bending it back.

"Yes!" the chieftain shrieked. "I'm sorry. I'll never do it again. Please." He looked out to everyone in the crowd. "I promise. I won't lay a hand on anyone ever again. I swear!"

Linus smiled and let go of his hand. "That wasn't so hard, was it? Now we can all go back to being friends again." He pulled the chieftain to his feet, and dusted him off, then turned to me. I stood quickly.

"Shall we?" He reached for my arm, but I jumped back, unable to look at him. I tightly hugged the rifle, turned, and began walking away.

He followed behind me but didn't say anything for several minutes as we made our way back through the village. When we were finally alone, I stopped and turned to face him.

"Why did you do that?" I asked, my hands still trembling.

He noticed, and his smile faded. "I've met men like that before. Quite a few, where I'm from. I'm sorry you had to see that, but men like that only speak one language, and that's a threat of violence bigger than their own. Do you understand?"

I did understand. I wanted to do something like that myself almost every time I met the man. Every time his hand brushed against my arm or his gaze lingered on me for too long, and I felt sick to my stomach. I always had my knife with me if I needed it, and I would've taken great pleasure in burying it into his neck. So, why was I such a hypocrite with Linus? Why did I recoil from his touch like he was just as awful as the chieftain? I knew why.

"I'm sorry. I...I just didn't expect that from you. I thought you were so gentle that I wouldn't see you hurt someone like that. It scared me."

"Gentle and wouldn't hurt anyone, eh? I wish it were so. Maybe in another life, Taylor, but that's not the world you and I live in. The fact that I'm standing here before you now is all the proof you need that I'm not always a gentleman, that I'm a very different man when I need to be."

I felt like a fool. He was right, of course. It felt so obvious when he said it aloud. Had I used him to get the rifle? Had I cared about what might happen to him if he was caught helping me? Wasn't I ready to break his heart, and worse, if it meant rescuing the village from the snake? Could I do it still?

"I'm sorry." I ran over and hugged him around the neck with one arm, cradling the rifle in the other. I held on for a moment longer than I meant to before jerking away my arm and stepping back. "Thank you for standing up for that girl…and me."

His smile returned to his face. "Don't be so quick to thank me yet. I'm legendary for turning everything I touch into a mess." He looked up to the sky. "Well, that took longer than expected. Mind offering me a place to stay tonight?" His face reddened. "I mean…I don't mean…What I'm saying is *any* place. *Not* with you. I didn't mean you…necessarily."

"I'm sure my parents won't mind if you share a room with my brother, assuming you can handle him talking your ear off."

He rubbed his face, regaining his composure. "Do you think your mother could treat me to some of her lovely cooking and more of that cactus wine?"

"I'll put in a good word for you. Just…don't mention the snake, alright?"

"Didn't plan on it. No need." He pointed to the rifle cradled in my arm and held up the canister of ammunition in his other hand. "The beast's as good as dead already."

II

Despite Mother's incessant worship of PanTech, she seemed genuinely surprised, almost uncomfortable, to see Linus walk through the door behind me. For once, Father actually looked up from his papers, holding his pipe in his right hand, raising one brow, but saying nothing. After a moment of uncomfortable silence and a gentle nudge from Linus, I cleared my throat.

"Everyone, this is Linus, the man I told you I was going to see today. He'll be joining us for dinner, and sharing a room with Ferris tonight if that's alright."

Mother smiled. "Of course. I'm just starting on dinner, so it's no trouble to make extra. We're so honored to have you join us, Linus."

"Ma'am," Linus said, nodding.

Father turned his pipe around and pointed the stem in the direction of the rifle I was still cradling in my arms. I met his eyes, and I think he already knew what I was holding.

"This?" I asked rhetorically. "Linus was quite a hunter in his zone and asked if I'd join him for some hunting tomorrow. Never hurts to have more meat, right?"

Linus never wavered in his smile and just nodded along.

"Well, you're probably going to be disappointed, young man. PanTech thinned our deer population several years ago. It was too plentiful a source of food to satisfy them that our children were sufficiently underfed. Adversity creates character, and PanTech does love its half-starved children."

An uncomfortable silence filled the room once again, for even longer this time. Mother shot Father a look that would have knocked him out if it were a punch, or at least sent him flying from his chair.

Linus scratched the back of his head. "Yeah…we went through the same thing when I was young. I'll not apologize for PanTech, but for what it's worth, I'm sorry myself."

Mother nearly tripped over herself, running over and grabbing his hand. "Oh no. Please forgive my husband. His tongue is so sharp it cuts right out of his mouth sometimes when his lips can't hold it back."

Linus only laughed. "I have the opposite problem. I can't find the right words at the right time. It made me rely on my hands a time or two too many. Anyway, the man speaks the honest truth. I'm taking my personal time right now, so I'm not representing PanTech. Just myself." He pointed to Father's pipe. "And, is that an honest to goodness smoking pipe in your hand? I haven't seen one of those in years."

Father's glare at Linus only hardened, but then he looked at me, and something in his eyes softened instantly, and he actually smiled. "I bet you haven't tried anything like this before. I have a second pipe if you'd care to join me while my wife makes dinner. My son never cared for it, so it'll be nice to have someone to smoke with."

I shook my finger at him. "That's because Mother wouldn't ever let me try it. I think it smells wonderful."

Mother let go of Linus and shook her own finger at me. "Ladies don't partake in such hobbies, Taylor."

I started to argue with her, but Linus's laughing drowned me out. "Yes, ma'am," he finally said.

I elbowed him in the ribs, but quickly pulled my arm back, rubbing it. Should've remembered the armor.

This only set Linus to laughing again, and he had to brace himself against the wall. It seemed even *he* had his limit to laughs and smiles, but when our eyes met, what I saw looked more like pain than happiness.

Father chuckled and stood to his feet. "What can I do, Tay, being so outnumbered?" He shrugged and disappeared around the corner, presumedly to retrieve the pipe and smoke weed jars.

My brother appeared around the corner, using the wall for support, his face covered in sweat. Mother rushed over to him, helping to hold him up.

"You shouldn't be up," she said. "The doctor said you needed at least a few more days of bed rest. Go on back to your room, and I'll bring you your dinner soon."

"Come on, Mother, you'll embarrass me in front of our guest here. You honestly expect me to sit in there when you guys are having all the fun out here? I can be in pain out here just as easily as I can in there, but with more conversation. The doctor's just being overly cautious. Just help me to my chair, if you don't mind."

She started to protest but realized how pointless that would be and helped him into his chair as he'd asked. He took a deep breath and let it out in a slow and exaggerated exhale. "Linus, was it? I'm Taylor's brother, Ferris. It's a good thing you picked Taylor. Otherwise, we'd be rivals for all the other pretty girls in the village, and I don't like your chances."

I felt my cheeks burning. I should've expected this from Ferris. Of course, he wouldn't let a little pain get in the way of embarrassing me. "Ferris!"

Linus broke out into laughter again before he'd fully recovered and had to stumble over and sit in one of the chairs at the table. "Since I did you such a big favor, maybe you could do one for me and put in a good word with your sister for me?"

Ferris grinned. "Not a chance."

Father returned with the extra pipe, already filled with smoke weed, handing it to Linus.

"Use the candle to light it. Just make a circle and puff it slowly. Careful, it may catch you off guard at first."

Linus eyed him incredulously and took two deep puffs as he moved the candle but dropped the candle before simultaneously picking it back up and nearly choking to death. He coughed and wheezed for several seconds while Father just grinned, and Mother looked absolutely petrified in horror.

At last, he caught his breath. "Wow!" he shouted. "This isn't tobacco!"

"Tobacco?" Father asked. "I wouldn't know. Is that what it was called in your zone?"

"That's what we smoked, but definitely not the same stuff," Linus said, still fighting off the remaining small coughs. He tried again, but much more slowly this time, finally getting a good light on his pipe. He puffed it cautiously, nodding to my father. "Some of the boys back home would get a real kick out of this stuff. They thought ours was strong."

Father only smiled and nodded, puffing his own, leaning back in his chair. "What was it like, in your zone? We seldom hear about the others."

Almost never? Try just never. Perhaps Father didn't want to deter him by saying we'd never heard anything beyond rumors of the other zones or overheard short conversations between soldiers.

Linus looked up at the ceiling like he was trying to recall something that happened a hundred years ago. "Well...I guess not too much different from this place, really. They tell us not to talk about it because it's a life we're supposed to leave behind completely. For most of PanTech's employees, this isn't too hard. Who would miss an adversity zone when you never have to worry about adversity again? Food of every kind you can imagine, medicine like you wouldn't believe, technology...," he trailed off, stopped, then took a puff of his pipe. "Sorry, that's not what you asked."

Linus paused again, taking a deep breath. "I lived in the desert too. Technology, I think, was probably on a similar level to your zone. We had horses. Big animals we rode on, like your camels, but shorter hair, and a lot more of them. Just about all of us had guns, like the one Taylor brought in. We even had smaller ones you could hold in one hand, with a revolving cylinder that held the rounds. That was my gun of choice. Something like the sidearm I'm carrying now, but not nearly as advanced." He patted the holster on his side that held the smaller gun soldiers always carried.

Ferris had been sitting quietly, for once, listening with his full attention. "You think all of the adversity zones are like ours? Do you know how many there are?"

Linus shook his head. "No idea how many there are, but there are quite a few. PanTech has the resources to manage a lot of them if they wanted to. One soldier told me that his zone was a city, where they spoke through something attached to a wire, and another person could hear them a long way away. They could have a box sitting on a table, and singing voices would come out, or PanTech would sometimes make announcements through them. I've seen things a lot more advanced since PanTech employed me, but I haven't been to any of their military facility much over the past year. Of course, the stuff I'm wearing is the most advanced thing I've seen yet, but I'm told that doesn't hold a candle to the things they have at the universities." He shot me a glance before lowering his head, slipping back into deep thought again.

Is that where the snake came from? One of PanTech's advanced universities, made in some lab with advanced technology and used to prey upon an adversity zone. I couldn't even begin to imagine all the good that could be accomplished from such a place. My father only had supplies and our lesser technology, and he'd invented things to improve our lives here before they stopped him. What's the point of having all of this technology and food if all you're going to use it for is to make everyone's life worse? None of this new information really changed anything. It just reinforced what we'd already suspected. PanTech is as sinister as they come.

"That sounds wonderful," Mother said, looking between Ferris and me. "Don't you want to pass your exam and be placed at one of them? You could study animal medicine, Taylor. Imagine all of the things you could do for humanity."

"Sure," I said. "I bet I could come up with new ways to starve people. I could take an animal that they depend on to eat and make its flesh poisonous. Or, maybe I could take a small animal they keep for pets and mess with their head, so they sneak into homes and kill babies. Imagine the endless possibility."

"Your disrespect really has no limit, I—"

"Mmm, what's that smell?" Linus interrupted. "Smells even better than the bread I had earlier."

"Oh, that's because it's much better fresh," she said. "It's actually the same bread. I'll bet it's done." She turned around, opened the door of the oven, and pulled out the pan. She sat it carefully onto the counter and sliced off equal portions for all of us, placing them on plates and setting them in front of us.

Ferris knocked a knuckle against Linus's armor. "You want to change out of that stuff? You could borrow some of my clothes. Can't be comfortable."

He grinned. "Quite the opposite. The whole thing's designed for comfort and cleans itself on the inside. It has to be drained and refilled about once a week, but it keeps us cool out here. All that, and it could still take a direct hit from your village's rifle, no problem."

Ferris just scrunched up his chin and nodded several times before taking a bite of his bread. It was nothing special to us, but clearly, Linus enjoyed it since he very reluctantly asked for seconds.

Once we'd all finished and spent a bit more time talking, we all retired to our rooms for the night. I could hear Ferris and Linus talking on and off into the deep hours of the night.

Tomorrow, we'd begin our hunt.

12

Linus and I were up early the next morning, before anyone else. I guess neither of us got much sleep. When I stepped into the common area, he was sitting at the table alone, his mind off in another place. Something about him looked sad and distant. He was so absorbed in whatever he was thinking about that he didn't even notice me until I pulled the chair to sit down at the table, and he jumped a bit.

"Well, good morning, Sunshine," he said in a low voice.

"You're the one with the golden hair. Shouldn't you be Sunshine?" I retorted.

He tapped his chin, mulling this over. "I see your point, but I don't think it suits me. Kind of a feminine nickname. Some of the boys I rode with used to call each other that to try to goad a reaction."

"Well, you have golden hair, blue eyes, and you're always smiling and laughing, so I think it's a fitting description."

He smiled, almost on cue. "Okay, you got me, but I'd still prefer it if you didn't call me that."

I held up my hands in surrender. "If you insist."

He continued smiling, and just stared at me for a moment. I waited because it looked as though he wanted to say something. "I think those clothes suit you. Do you mind if I say that?"

If he hadn't asked if it was okay for him to say it…and after he'd already said it, I might've blushed. Instead, I laughed and pressed my hand over my mouth to keep from waking everyone else. "No, you can't say it. How will you take it back?"

His smile faded, and he frowned slightly. "Oh. Umm...," he looked away. "Sorry. You're just so beautiful, and I just said it without thinking and oh...man, I just did it again. Sorry."

This time, I did blush. Hard. "Oh, I was only kidding. I don't mind if you say it. I...uh...."

He scratched his head and stood up. "Well, are you ready to—"

"I think you are too," I blurted. I was so focused on finishing the sentence that I talked right over him. I expected him to get all flustered again, but he didn't. Instead, for just a moment, he looked as sad and distant as he did when I'd first stepped over to the table, as though he was remembering the death of a friend. Perhaps he was. "And, yes. I'm ready."

He pushed in his chair and signaled for me to walk over to the door, which he opened and held for me. I stared at him blankly for a moment.

"Oh...," he started. "This is a custom where I'm from. A man often holds the door for women. It's...hmm...a show of respect."

"Oh," I said, raising a brow. "Sounds...kind of strange. Can the women not open doors where you're from because of some kind of rule?"

He laughed. "No, Taylor. You know what," he said, stepping back from the door and letting it close. "I think you can handle this door."

I grinned but immediately wished I'd just humored him and walked out the door. Now he looked embarrassed again. I liked this Linus more than the one who felt like he had to hurt people, and I think he liked this part of himself too. The one that smiled and got rosy cheeks when he complimented me and got flustered when he tripped up on his words. And, in that moment, I hated the world that forced a man like him into a life of violence. PanTech's world.

I picked up my pack, and struggled for a moment to fit it on my back, then slung the rifle over my shoulder. It took some trial and error, but I finally remembered how to load the magazine last night, so all I had to do was chamber the round with the bolt, and I'd be ready to go.

I pointed to the goggles on my head and the mask hanging around my neck. "Does your helmet protect you from the sand if the wind picks up today?"

He nodded. "Sure does. Don't worry about me. I'll keep it strapped on my waist until I need it, though. I hate that thing."

I smiled and pushed open the door but was startled by two PanTech soldiers standing just a few feet outside of it. I stumbled back and was caught by Linus, who didn't seem surprised at all.

The soldier on the left was taller and bigger than Linus and looked several years his senior. His skin was reddish-brown, and his hair was dark and long, resting even with his shoulders. The soldier on the right was pale, with red hair. I recognized him as the jerk who bullied the elderly woman before the commander gave her speech. I'd give anything to dump a bucket of angry terror ants on his head.

He was the first to speak.

"You didn't return to the camp last night, Linus," he said.

I stepped to the side so that I wouldn't be between them and so I could watch all of them.

Linus grinned. "I think you're right. As usual, you're a master of the obvious. Pretty sure I didn't have to."

"I'm pretty sure the rules state—"

"Oh, go choke on the rules, Peter, but I doubt it'll make the commander like you any better."

Peter reached for his sidearm, but the bigger man put his hand on his arm, stopping him.

"Better thank Oscar here for stopping you. I'd have blown you away before you got it out of the holster," Linus said, grinning, resting his own hand on his sidearm, tapping his finger on it a few times, but not taking his eyes off Peter.

Oscar took a step forward and put himself between the two of them. "Cut it out, Linus. You know we're just doing our job. The commander sent us to check up on you is all, and that's all we're doing. You know she has a short fuse, though, so please stop pushing everyone. Every commanding officer has had enhancements performed, and you know that, so if you pull the same thing with her again like you enjoy doing with everyone else, she could shoot you five times before you drew your gun, even if you were the fastest human ever to live. Take it from someone with a few years of experience on you. Let that rebellious spark of yours burn out while you still can."

Linus gritted his teeth. It was the first time he actually looked angry since I met him. Even when he was dealing with the chieftain, he was smiling. He wasn't now.

"Noted, but I didn't ask to be a soldier."

Oscar sighed. "No, but you were *allowed* to be one. Don't forget that. You're on your last strike." He nodded to

Peter before Linus could answer, and the two of them walked out of the village.

Linus still stood there, his jaw tight over clenched teeth.

"Are you okay? And what did they mean by you being on your last strike?" I asked, hugging his arm. "Are you going to get in trouble just for being here overnight?"

He finally managed to force a smile back onto his face. "You don't need to concern yourself with that, so please don't ask about it again. That's some personal business of mine I'd rather not get into…and no, I'm not going to get in trouble just for being here overnight. That rule is in place because usually, a soldier doesn't have as much downtime saved up as I do. It's never enforced. Peter just used it to take a jab at me. Don't worry." He took a deep breath and sighed. "Ready to hunt?"

I let go of his arm, not really buying his explanation, but thinking it'd be better not to push the conversation further. "I'm ready."

I wondered if they'd go back and tell their commander about the rifle I had. Everyone employed by PanTech, even the soldiers, was much more intelligent than the average person. They all had to pass the exam to be selected. Would they put everything together and realize I was hunting the snake and that Linus was helping me? Surely, he was forbidden from something like that, wasn't he?

"Good, I need to take out some frustration on something. May as well be a giant snake with super armored scales."

My eyes went wide. "Super arm—" I shook my head. "Did you just say it had super armored scales?" I asked, unable to override my urge to shout.

He put his finger over his lips to shush me and looked around, making sure no one had heard me. Thankfully, we were alone.

"Yeah, I might have failed to mention that part, huh? Relax. I'm pretty sure that rifle will still penetrate it, but a sword or spear probably won't."

I furrowed my brow, glaring at him. "Any other superpowers you'd like to tell me about before we're standing out there trying to kill the thing?"

"Well...," he started. "I don't actually know. I only overheard the scales part. I'm not even sure that's accurate, but it didn't sound like a joke when I heard it." He smiled again, reaching down to tap his sidearm. "Even if your rifle doesn't do it, my blaster will take care of it. But, if the blaster fails, my rifle could take down any living thing anywhere on Earth. But, you can also hear the thing being fired almost anywhere on Earth, and even though my helmet protects my hearing, you may go deaf if I shoot the thing while you're standing next to me."

And, they'll come to see why you fired, I finished for him inside my head.

"Fine. I trust you. Let's get out of the village before we talk about it anymore."

I should've known I'd lose my nerve. Not about the snake. I was ready for anything with the snake, but not with Linus. Before, I was prepared to sacrifice him to take care of the snake and save the village. Why did it suddenly weigh so heavily on me that he might get in serious trouble? Didn't I know from the beginning that he would? Hadn't I expected it?

We had only made it about a hundred yards out of the village and were still within sight when I took a deep breath and let it out. "Stop," I said firmly.

He wheeled around, looking in both of our side directions rapidly. "What, did you see something?" he asked, putting his hand on his blaster's grip.

"Uh...no! Sorry...," I trailed off. "I just...you don't have to do this, you know."

He narrowed his eyes at me. "Yeah, I know. And?"

"Well, it's just...," I looked down, trying to hide the tears starting to well in my eyes. *Really? Now you're going to get all emotional, Taylor? Face it. You're falling hard for this guy. Give me a break.* "Those soldiers sounded serious. What if they figure out that you're out here hunting that snake with me? You're going to get in trouble. Just...go back to your camp. You said yourself that this rifle should do the job."

"Yeah, I said it *should* do the job. Also, this is my door, Taylor."

I tilted my head at him. "Your...door?"

He nodded. "You know how you said earlier that holding open the door for women didn't make sense because they can open doors too? Well, I'm perfectly capable of deciding whether or not I want to go on this hunt with you. I know the risks far better than you do, so just banish those thoughts from your mind. They're silly, and you'll just blame yourself if something happens. I'm out here hunting it with you because it's something *I* want to do. I'll decide what's good for me, and PanTech can go shove it where the sun don't shine if they've got a problem with that. Got it?"

I furrowed my brow, hating to ruin the serious moment, but he'd lost me. "Shove what? Where the sun doesn't shine…you mean, like in the shade?"

He exploded into laughter and laughed so hard that he collapsed onto his hands and knees. Finally, he looked up at me, his lips pressed into a forced smile in order to hold back the laughter still trying to escape. He struggled to his feet, dusting the sand off his armor. "I'm not about to explain that one to you. Now, come on. We've got a giant, armored snake to kill."

13

We'd continued walking for a while until we were out of sight of the village and in the opposite direction of the PanTech camp.

"It's entirely possible this thing has moved on. Do you think we could be that lucky?" I asked.

"It hasn't moved on," he replied, a little too quickly.

I stopped, looking at him. "How are you so certain of that?"

"I helped bring it here, remember? We were all briefed on what to expect and how to…guide the thing, in a way."

He continued walking, and I had no choice but to continue walking with him.

"What do you mean by 'guide' it?"

He looked up at the sun briefly before rubbing sweat from his forehead. "It's hot enough to melt steel out here."

"Linus."

"Yeah?" He said, finally stopping to look at me.

"What do you mean by controlling it?"

"I didn't say control. I said guide," he grinned.

I punched him in the arm. Ouch. "Come on. You're going this far. Why keep anything from me at this point?"

He sighed, pointing at a rock where we could catch a bit of shade. We walked over to it, and he sat down, patting the sand beside him. I sat next to him.

"It's not that…well…not that I'm *keeping* things from you, exactly. I'm just a little embarrassed, is all."

I chuckled, shaking my head. "I can't tell from one minute to the next what's going to embarrass you, make you angry, or make you laugh."

He smiled, running his fingers through his now sweaty hair. "Am I really that unpredictable?"

"Not really," I conceded. "I just need to get to know you better, or maybe I'm just making an excuse to get to know you better."

He put his arm around my shoulders and pulled me closer to him. "I'll take it, then."

We sat silently for a few minutes, less awkwardly than I'd expected.

"So, 'guide' how?"

He sighed, hanging his head. "PanTech set it up so that it can't escape. It has implants. One of which won't let it outside of a certain radius, within a sort of triangle-shaped area of the camp, where the camp is the point of that triangle."

"So that's why they're set up at the edge of the boundary…," I added.

He nodded. "Yep. You got it. And, as you probably already guessed, that range extends to just about the edge of the opposite boundary."

"Has it been trained to hunt humans?" I asked, bracing myself against the answer.

"Yeah…," he said, still not looking up.

"How…did they accomplish that?"

"Don't know, but I'm afraid to let my imagination fill in the blanks. Would caution you against the same thing," he said.

"Are they that cruel or that advanced?"

He raised his head and tapped his chin, genuinely considering this for a moment. "I'd say advanced. Based on my experience, they really do think they're doing the right thing and what's best for everyone."

"What about you?" I asked.

"You're kidding...," he frowned, looking genuinely wounded by the question.

"Sorry, dumb question, considering you're out here," I conceded.

He shook his head. "I guess I couldn't disagree completely that having a harder life makes us better people, but I think I'd rather be free and happy than 'better,' whatever that means. There was my dad, then my mom, and then a brief period of time where I wanted freedom so bad that I chose the freedom to do bad things. It's a little sad, I think, that I look back on those memories as my best. I thought with PanTech it would be different. I gave in and took their test, scored well, got accepted to an engineering school. Still, almost immediately, they considered me problematic. I argued with everything, snooped around in places I wasn't supposed to, and got on the bad side of every instructor I had. Ended up being sent off to the military division to learn discipline, but I didn't do a lot better there. Got into a fight my first day I was over there and got assigned to what they call 'low-tech' zones. No offense, but that's where they send their bottom-of-the-barrel people. Expectations are low, and this group is reduced to bullying people with sticks and rocks, maybe the occasional sword. Not that it makes any difference. Wrong is wrong no matter how hard it is to bully a zone successfully."

I kept quiet, just nodding as he ranted, not expecting the sudden openness.

"I'm no fan of PanTech, but my brother always felt like we could help change it from the inside if we passed our exam."

He shrugged. "Maybe, but that's not for me. I don't have that kind of patience or care for the world."

Now I regretted asking him about this in the first place. This conversation obviously wasn't good for his state of mind.

"So, about the super-armored snake...."

He perked up. "Yeah? What are you thinking?"

I scratched my neck and looked around. "I was actually wanting to ask what *you* were thinking. I have no idea how to bait one this huge without leading out big game. We can't afford to sacrifice any more livestock or camels. Also, since it travels underground, it could be anywhere within that triangle you mentioned."

He grinned. "Why, Taylor, I'm disappointed in you. You dragged me all the way out here without a plan?"

I lightly punched him in the arm. "*You* dragged *yourself* out here, remember? You keep saying so."

His grin stretched even wider. "Well, I hope this doesn't surprise you, but I actually *do* have a plan."

As much as I wanted to tease him, I wasn't surprised at all.

"Care to enlighten me?" I asked.

"PanTech needs to have a way to direct this creature where they want it, besides holding it within the radius I already mentioned. If they want to guide it to a specific spot in the village, say a secret meeting house for rebels, they wanted a way to summon it there. Otherwise, it wouldn't be much of a weapon."

"Let me guess," I said. "Special bait that brings the beast in quickly. I'm guessing something to make it extra hungry and extra violent."

He nodded several times. "Wow, Taylor. I knew you'd guess the first part, but not the second."

"Wait...I was right?" I glared at him. "It makes it extra hungry and violent..., and we *actually* want to use that to bring the snake here? Isn't it going to be hard enough to kill already without it going berserk? I was hoping we could sneak up on it and kill it while it was eating, the way you can with the small ones."

"Look," he said before sighing. "I get where you're coming from, but otherwise, we'll have to wander around aimlessly and wait for the thing to strike again. It won't be a pig next time, Taylor. It'll be a villager. It could be your parents. It could be your friend. It could be a child. If that's not bad enough, I'll run out of my personal time soon. I'm afraid if we don't do this now, you'll have to fight it alone. I do not want to risk that. I'd rather die killing it than to let you do this on your own."

My eyes went wide, and I felt myself blushing again.

"I'm not going to let it kill you, either, Mr. Hero. This rifle isn't for show."

He nodded. "Yeah, it's not. Alright, partner, are you ready to get this party started?"

"Ready as I'll ever be," I said.

He pulled a small box from his pack and stood to his feet.

He started to open it but just rested his hand on top, looking back at me. "I suspect Peter and Oscar, the two soldiers who paid me a visit this morning, realized one of these was missing and was hoping to catch me with it. That's why I went out of my way to make sure Peter lost his cool, and Oscar would have to back him off. They're not going to give up easily, but by the time they realize I really do have it, it'll be too late. Just avoid them, or play as stupid as possible, no matter what. Don't be fooled into cooperating with them, no matter what. Especially Oscar. He always seems to know the right thing to say to pull confessions out of people. Don't trust Oscar, no matter what he says. No matter what he offers you."

I nodded. "Alright, I'll remember that."

"Promise me," he said, his voice becoming harder than before.

"Okay, I promise," I said reluctantly. I wanted to ask him why I had to promise, but I knew I wouldn't get anything more out of him right now. "I'm ready when you are."

He closed his eyes and took a deep breath, looking up to the sky. Then, he smiled, opened the box, and reached inside. What he pulled out wasn't anything spectacular. I'm not sure what I was expecting. Maybe a machine that produces sound, or an insect with a pheromone that the snake was attracted to. This was nothing but a small pellet, and it looked like some of the compressed feed we used for some of our livestock. He placed it back into the box without closing the lid. He pulled out his canteen, opened the lid, and offered it to me.

"Drink?" he asked.

I took it from his hand and indulged in a small drink before handing it back to him. "Kind of small…isn't it?"

He looked at me and grinned before turning his attention to the box and pellet. "I was hoping you'd say that." He held his open canteen over the box and began tilting it before stopping and looking at me, his smile wide. "You might want to take a few steps back."

I did, and he began pouring water into the box, then tossed it quite a way away from us. It sizzled, then a foam shot out of it, covering the large area around it before soaking into the sand.

"Now?" I asked.

"Now, we wait. How long depends on how far it is away from us right now, but when it shows up, be prepared to give it all you have."

I unwrapped my rifle, pulled the bolt back toward me, and then pushed it forward again to ready a round into the chamber. I used my left hand to pull the goggles down over my eyes and stretched the scarf over my mouth.

"Aren't you going to put your helmet on?" I asked.

"Nope."

"Nope? Nope, why?"

"Because if I secure it on the suit, they'll be able to monitor what I say. No thanks. I'm used to the desert too, remember? I'll be fine. This foam will keep it from stirring up too much dust when it emerges."

I pulled down my scarf. "You're not big on giving information up front, are you?"

"You like me anyway, right?" he winked.

"I think I do unless there's something else you'd like to tell me that you've been holding back on?"

"Well, I wouldn't mind...," he began, then shook his head. "No, never mind."

He reached down and unholstered his sidearm, kneeling down and putting his hand on the sand. He stayed like this for several minutes, neither of us wanting to speak.

"Maybe...it didn't work?" I asked.

He just kept staring down, his hand pressed firmly into the sand. "Yeah, maybe I was supposed to take it out of the box first, or maybe I put too much—"

His thoughts were interrupted by a slow rumble. At first, subtle enough that I wasn't sure if I'd felt it correctly. He bent down further, pressing his ear to the ground, holding up one finger.

"False alarm?" I whispered.

He waited a few more minutes before letting out a big sigh of relief. "Looks like it's going to be a—"

He was interrupted again, and this time there was no mistake. The ground quaked beneath us, and I stumbled to my knees, holding the rifle with my right hand and steadying myself with my left. Linus leapt to his feet, pressing in some kind of mechanism on his sidearm, and it let out a low hum.

"It's about to emerge. Get ready!" he shouted before I noticed the smile return to his face. He wasn't dreading this at all or terrified like I was. He was looking forward to it. He was excited.

With a muffled thud and a splattering of the foam covering the ground, the demon emerged into the open air.

14

Nothing I could have done, no thought that could have entered my mind, and no amount of preparation or training could have made me ready for this moment. Seeing this creature now, in its massive size and power, made me freeze in place. I could only stare, my mouth agape, my legs being sapped of their strength to hold me up. I wanted to run, to hide or to lock myself away in the safety of my home.

"Taylor!" Linus shouted.

I barely heard him and didn't register what he was saying. I could only watch the snake slowly move around us, ten times the size I imagined it. How could PanTech do this to us? This would have killed everyone. It's going to kill us....

"Taylor! Listen to me," Linus pleaded. "You've got to snap out of it. If you don't, you're dead. It had blood. It bleeds, and anything that bleeds, dies. You're going to make it die, and I'm going to help you. Lift your rifle, aim, and fire before it makes it all the way out. I'll cover you while you reload."

I snapped my attention back to reality, but my hands shook like a sheet of paper in the wind. I gasped and pulled in the deepest breath I could, then let it out. I did it again and again until, at last, I could open and close my hands and ignore the tears streaming down my face. I raised my rifle and fired the first few shots. The first two missed, but the third hit. I could tell it hadn't penetrated deeply. It took me a moment to realize I still had seven rounds in the magazine. It coiled close around me and fixated on my position. I shot the last seven shots in rapid succession, only about half hitting.

"It's going to kill me!" I screamed.

"No, it won't," Linus said, as calmly as he could. "I'll hit it as it strikes. It'll pull back. Reload. Now. This sidearm isn't rapid fire."

I dropped to my knees and pulled out a loaded magazine with ten fresh rounds, dropped the other magazine before throwing it into my pack, and slammed the bolt forward. As I did, the snake struck toward me with blinding speed. Still true to his word, Linus fired his blaster and hit the side of its head, sending it recoiling back and facing its attention toward him now. Blood was oozing from the much larger wound on the side of its head. I could tell from looking at it that it wasn't even close to being dead. We'd made a huge mistake. We were going to die here, and it was all my fault.

I raised my rifle and, more calmly this time, fired another ten rounds into its neck, opposite the side Linus had shot. It turned its attention to me again.

Now Linus looked panicked. "Come on. Come on, come on, come on!" The low hum came from his blaster. It needed time. I would have to load the rounds one at a time into an empty magazine now, and we were helpless in this moment. "Sling the rifle, grab some ammo, and reload as you run around it. We need to make it harder for it to zero in on one of us. I'll go the opposite way. Move!"

His last command was jarring in its harshness, and I did as he instructed. I released the magazine and slung the rifle, grabbed a handful of the ammunition, and struggled over the snake's back to make my circle around. Linus did the same but punched it as he did, making sure it paid the most attention to him. Just as he made it over the snake's back, it struck at him blindingly fast, and Linus dashed forward with equally impressive speed, narrowly escaping the strike. It was beyond human, and only the armor could have explained it. I pulled my attention away from him, and frantically tried to load rounds into the magazine while running, which was harder than I would have ever expected it to be. I dropped the first several before I finally got the hang of it. I'd managed to load in seven. The rest were lost in the sand.

I stopped, took a deep breath, and held the rifle up steady to my shoulder, pressing my cheek into it. I held my breath, and fired all seven shots. Slower, this time. I took the time to aim more carefully, even as the snake snapped its head around and repositioned its body to face me fully. I was calmer, slower, more careful. More precise. All seven shots hit the target and all in the neck near the others.

Linus punched it several times, trying to get its attention, but it didn't work this time. The snake shot toward me, and all I had time to do was hold up the rifle vertically so it couldn't close its powerful jaws and use its fangs to pull me into its stomach. I could feel the hot breath as it closed down on the rifle. It flung its head about frantically, trying to dislodge the rifle, knocking me through the air and landing hard on the ground, forcing all of the air to leave my lungs. My first gasp was filled with sand, which only made things worse. It was stirring up more and more sand now as it thrashed about. Finally, the rifle went sailing into a different direction. Fortunately, I saw where it landed, and pulled my scarf over my mouth and my goggles over my eyes. Linus would have a hard time now.

It came back for another attempt, but this time Linus was there between us, and fired the shot from his blaster at the last possible moment, doing the most possible damage. This time, a large chunk of its face was exposed, and one of its eyes was completely useless. This shot would have killed most mammals, but reptiles are more resilient creatures. They can take far more damage.

It flung itself backward and slammed onto the ground several times, sending Linus to his hands and knees from the small quake it had created.

We were especially vulnerable now. It took nearly a minute to charge that shot, and I didn't have any ammunition nor a rifle to load it in.

"You have to get up. Get your rifle back, and load another magazine. I have an idea, but you have to trust me. Go!" Linus shouted, before coughing on the sand that was coating his throat. His blaster hummed as it recharged again, a steady stream of smoke rising from it now. Was it overheating?

I jumped to my feet and made a run for the rifle. Linus ran with me this time, instead of in the opposite direction. I didn't understand why until we made it to the rifle. I knew it was here…somewhere, but I couldn't see it anymore. The sand must have covered it. I dropped to my hands and knees and started digging for it.

"I don't see it!" I screamed. "I can't find it. I can't see it," I said, losing my nerve again, feeling myself crying.

"Take a deep breath. It's there. Don't worry about anything except finding it," he said, positioning himself between the snake and me.

It raised its head again, and steadied itself, then struck at Linus. He grabbed onto one of the fangs with his left arm and stomped his foot into the bottom of its mouth. At first, I thought he would have the strength to rip its jaw apart, but he couldn't spread it open that far. He tried twisting the fang, but it had little effect beyond making the snake sway a bit. It hissed loudly and strained to collapse its jaws onto Linus. The power armor wasn't enough to match the snake's strength, and he slowly began to bend with the snake's effort, the point of the opposite fang resting on his shoulder. Though, he held firmly to his blaster with his right hand, refusing to abandon it.

None of this helped me to calm myself, but after a moment of digging, I finally managed to find the gun beneath the sand. I picked it up and ran toward my bag where the ammunition was, released the magazine, and began reloading, despite my hands trembling even more than before. I looked over my shoulder to see Linus clenching his jaw and growling in pain. The snake's fang had cracked through the shoulder of his armor, and the clear fluid that filled it was pouring out, tinged with red blood.

I slammed the bolt forward and ran back to him, stopping and firing ten more shots into the snake's neck, hoping against all hope that it would be enough to kill it once and for all.

It wasn't.

Blood poured from its many wounds, but it didn't seem to weaken it in the slightest, only angering it more. It picked up Linus and began thrashing around again. His blaster should have been charged by now, but it wasn't. Something must be wrong with it. Smoke billowed from it now, as if it were about to explode, but Linus held a death grip on it nonetheless. The snake weakened enough that it wasn't able to keep him up in the air anymore. I tried to release the magazine, but it was stuck. I tried as hard as I could to yank it out, but it wouldn't budge. I threw down the rifle and pulled out my knife, running and leaping onto the snake's head, stabbing into the already wounded areas, knowing the knife couldn't penetrate the undamaged scales. It did well enough in sabotaging the existing wounds.

It flung its head to the side, sending me flying through the air again.

The hum coming from the blaster was high-pitched now, and it shook violently in his hand. "Get back, Taylor! Run!" He shouted while slamming the gun into his bent knee, activating the charging mechanism again. He'd done this three times now, without firing it. Was he overloading it? I scrambled to my feet, barely able to keep my balance, and began to scoot myself back through the sand, further away. Linus threw the gun into the snake's throat, freeing his right hand to grasp the other fang. He roared and forced its mouth open with all his strength, but it wasn't enough. He couldn't pull the fang the final few inches from his armor. Ignoring his pleas, I ran back to the snake again, jamming my knife deep into its eye. It opened its mouth reflexively, and Linus was finally able to free himself from the fang completely.

He grabbed me in his arms and ran a few steps before falling, sending both of us collapsing to the ground. The snake raised its head again, readying for another strike. Linus rolled on top of me, shielding my body with his. As the snake twitched to move forward, I could hear an explosion, and a flash of light came from its mouth. Pieces of its flesh flew in all directions, as well as fragments of the blaster, like bullets thudding against the sand.

The snake fell to the ground with a thud. Its body coiled tightly for a moment, then went limp.

Linus pushed himself up off me and gave me a smile before rolling off to the side, onto his back.

"Have fun?" he asked, holding his shoulder and grimacing.

I raised my goggles and pulled down my mask, wiping my face. "I'm snotting everywhere, and my goggles are all fogged up from crying like a scared little girl. I thought I could be brave, but when it came right down to it, I was so scared I almost ran away."

He laughed but abruptly stopped and winced. "I think I'd call that normal. Don't sweat it. Oh, and thanks for saving me back there. Good thing you didn't run, or I'd be dead meat."

"Save...save you?" I said, more angry than surprised. "Linus, you are the worst liar of all the men I've ever met."

He managed something like a half-grin while gritting his teeth. "Guess maybe I'm not your type after all, then."

I smiled and threw my arms around his neck, kissing him deeply. He relaxed at first, pushing his lips into mine. He made a few grunting noises while tapping my shoulder before I realized my elbow was directly over his wound, pressing my full weight into it.

"Oh...sorry!" I said, feeling as though my skin was going to melt off my face. I can't believe I did that. But, wow. Just wow.

"Of all the things in the world a person should apologize for, *that* should go at the bottom of the list. Come on. Let's get you back home."

15

It was only about midday when we made it back to the village. At first, I thought we'd be able to make it back to my house before the gawkers gathered around, but I was wrong. Some were well-meaning, offering to help us. One man took Linus's other arm over his shoulder and helped me support him as we walked. Others, I think, were just enjoying the novelty of an injured PanTech soldier, but there was a little more than that. There were still others, unless I was mistaken, who almost looked excited by it. Not that I could blame them, with everything PanTech represented.

I wished I had the time to stop and explain to each and every one of them how Linus was different. How he was heroic, and wanted to help people and make their lives better. How he stood up for others and for himself. How he liked those who valued freedom and how he'd risked harsh punishment and his own life just to experience what little of it he could. I wanted to tell them how I hated PanTech too, and how Linus was on our side...but I didn't know how much of that was true, and almost nothing is that black and white. Here he was, having joined them, wearing full PanTech battle armor, visiting adversity zones to make sure things were hard enough for us to become *better* than we'd be without them. *Better* than we'd be if we had enough to eat, enough medicine, and safety. No. It would be wasted words, and I had a feeling Linus didn't particularly care.

When we arrived at my house, I thanked the stranger for helping us but thought it better to send him away. Once inside, I sat Linus down at the table in the common room.

Only after he'd sat down did I realize how much he was bleeding. The wound must have been deeper than I'd thought and that he'd let on.

"Please tell me that snake wasn't venomous," I said.

"Not that I know of." He tried to shrug, but could only manage it with one shoulder, immediately showing his regret for trying with a sharp wince.

"We need to get that armor off...right?" I asked, completely unsure of what to do. I'd never seen damaged PanTech armor, much less a soldier not wearing it. All I'd seen was most of them without a helmet, but that was common. With all the liquid shooting out and an open wound, this was something completely different.

He chuckled, what little he could manage. "I wish I'd paid more attention when they told us how to handle this. Give me a minute to think about it."

Just then, my mother walked in and screamed. Ferris came limping into the room as well and put his hands on my mother's shoulders.

"What did you do, Taylor?" Mother shouted.

"What's that supposed—" I started, but Linus cut me off.

"I didn't listen to her and ended up falling onto a rock. A...uh...sharp rock that pierced my armor," he tried, as poor a liar as he was. But, no one questioned a PanTech soldier. Even though it was perhaps the least convincing lie of all time, and Linus probably knew it, my mother shut her mouth and didn't push the matter.

"Get my sewing kit, Mother. It's in my room, near the closet. The thread is thick, but it'll have to do."

She shook her head. "No. I have one with a more suitable thread for a wound. I'll go and fetch it."

Ferris limped over to us, obviously still in pain himself. "There were two PanTech soldiers who came by earlier looking for you, Linus. They said they'd be back later."

Linus only smiled and nodded.

"So, the armor?" I asked. I was sure those soldiers checking in on him again was an important detail but probably less important than say…staying alive.

"Right. Well, it's not as simple as just removing it. It's…," he stopped, scratching his chin. "It's attached. Pretty deeply, and anchored in. The wires are thin, so they could either break when we pull them, or they could be stubborn. I'm getting lightheaded, so I think I've lost too much blood already. You're going to have to remove the torso, at least."

I just blinked at him. This was a lot to take in. I could tell by the look on Ferris's face that he was thinking along the same lines.

"That does *not* sound very reassuring," I said.

He attempted another shrug with the same result. "Ouch…anyway, sorry, what do you want me to do? Bleed out? There are covers that overlay with the armor. If you lift them far enough, you'll find brackets that you'll be able to pull up on the end where the lip faces up a bit. I don't know how else to describe it, Taylor, and I don't mean to be pushy, but you're probably going to want to do this sooner than later, or I'm going to be unconscious."

Ferris didn't hesitate, pulling up the flaps where the arms connected with the torso, fiddling a moment, and producing a loud snapping sound that shook the armor. I followed his lead with the opposite side, and after a moment, we'd removed the arms.

Linus's arms were smaller than expected, probably because of the sheer bulk of the suit. They were lean and muscular and extremely pale, contrasting from his tanned face. He must've been in this thing for a while. He did mention that they didn't really take it off. Just changed out the fluid inside.

"Alright. Good work. Now you'll have to go up along each side doing the same thing. When both sides are unbuckled, you'll have to do a line around my waist. Then, you'll both have to grab the bottom near the waist and the top near my neck to pull the pieces away from one another...I think," he said.

Mother came back into the room but stood silently in the doorway, her face wracked with worry.

It took Ferris and I several minutes, but we managed to undo the buckles. We pulled the two pieces in opposite directions, but they didn't budge.

"You have to lift up on the front armor. Slide up, then out," Mother said. "I have the thread ready. I'll take care of his wound once the armor is off."

Ferris turned and looked at her for a moment, the confusion clear on his face, but she didn't offer anything to alleviate it.

"Ferris," I said, getting his attention back on the task at hand. "Ready?"

He nodded, and we pulled the pieces apart. The remaining fluid in the armor's torso spilled onto the floor, but it was completely red this time, compared to the mostly clear fluid I'd seen spill out earlier.

I dropped the armor's chest portion and moved to get a closer look at his wound. It wasn't wide, but it must've been deeper than we thought. It couldn't have gone as far as his lung, based on his breathing, but it could've been almost that far.

Mother stepped forward and began unraveling thread, but I snatched it from her hand.

"I'll do it," I said, as firmly as I could.

"He's not a camel, Taylor. He—"

"I trust Taylor with my life," Linus interrupted. "And then some." He scratched the back of his head. "But…would you mind too terribly rustling me up some grub?"

"Some…grub?" she asked, and this set him into a laughing fit, which continued for a minute despite the obvious pain it caused him.

"Food, ma'am. Sorry. Anything is good, but some of that wine would really hit the spot."

She stepped around us and began preparing a meal for him, as he'd asked.

I didn't waste any more time. The wound was still oozing blood, and his hunger was probably partly because of the blood he'd lost already. I sewed quickly and efficiently, but not gently. Linus barely batted an eye. I felt his muscle flinch under the needle a couple of times, but he never protested or made a sound. He'd experienced this before. Maybe many times before. Realizing this made me sad. Was it pity?

No, not pity. Not exactly. It was realizing that he'd been through so much more than he'd let on, and he didn't have anyone to share his pain with him. Maybe I really did have it easy. Linus wasn't much older than me, but…looking at all of the scars that covered his torso, he'd seen so much more hardship than I had. Yet, he'd managed to hold onto some part of his soul and found a way to be kind. He never complained or made light of my troubles. His hardships had made him strong, resourceful, appreciative, and sometimes kind, but they'd also robbed him of love and happiness. PanTech didn't understand that.

He had deserved to be happy and to have food in his stomach and a warmth in his heart. He deserved to be loved, and I'd decided without a doubt that I wanted to give him my love in all the ways I could. Maybe he could retire to the village at the end of his service, or I could pass my exam and ask to be assigned to the same group as him, or….

Realization slammed into me, like closing a romantic book midway through, that PanTech would never allow this to happen. But, maybe…just maybe, I could continue to visit him while he was here. They visited at least once a month. If he saved up his personal time, and used it to spend time with me, just like he did today, then maybe—

"Taylor?" Linus asked, tilting his head and leaning down to look at my face. "You alright?"

I nodded, leaning in to look at the wounds along his sides. Several small wounds went up along his ribs, matching on both sides, where the wires embedded in his flesh had pulled out.

"I'm fine…but—"

"Mind if I borrow some of your clothes, Ferris? You're a little bigger than me, but baggy is good. Oh, and a poncho, like what you'd wear if you had to go out in the rain. And uh…a hat. May as well go all out. Widest brimmed hat you have."

Ferris nodded. "I usually just wear a wrap…but Father has some hats. I'm sure if he was willing to share a pipe, he won't mind if you borrow one of his hats."

"Where is Father?" I asked, irritated with myself that I'd only just now realized he wasn't home.

"He went out to deliver the lesson plans he'd been working on. Remember? He'll be going over them for a while. He won't be home for a few more hours, at least."

"Your rifle," Linus said, suddenly.

"What?" I asked, staring at him.

"Hand it to me. I'll need to fix the jam. We don't want to return a defective rifle, do we?" he smiled.

"Sure, but that can wait," I urged. "You can do it later, right?"

"Now," he said, holding out his arm with his hand open.

I handed him the rifle, and he pressed the magazine release, taking a couple of quick pulls before giving up. This wasn't good for his wound. At all.

"Linus, you can do this later. Please."

He ignored me and put the butt of the rifle stock down on the floor, pointing it up straight at the ceiling. He raised his leg and kicked the bolt. When it didn't move, he kicked it a second time, a little harder this time. A bullet ejected and flew across the room. He sat the rifle back in his lap, and this time the magazine fell out freely. He smiled and breathed a huge sigh of relief. Was he really that concerned with disappointing the chieftain? Or, maybe, he just didn't want to leave the village without a working rifle.

Ferris returned with the clothes, and Linus dressed quickly. He put on the long coat over his shirt, despite the weather. Didn't he say the suit kept him cool? Surely he was burning up with all of this on. Usually, when it rained, the weather was cooler. He fit the wide-brimmed hat on his head. He took it off again and just stared at it for a moment, before smiling.

"Not exactly what I'm used to wearing, but close enough," he said, putting it back on his head, and standing to his feet.

"Hey, what are you doing?" I asked.

Again, he ignored me. He placed the rifle inside his coat and leaned over, looking himself up and down, before nodding.

"Good enough."

Mother stepped over and sat a plate of meat and a cup of wine down in front of Linus, both of which he made short work of.

Linus stepped toward me and put his arm around me, holding the rifle beneath his coat with his other arm. He kissed me while Mother and Ferris competed for whose jaw would hit the floor first. He took a step back and gripped my shoulder.

"This is goodbye. Please don't say anything. Don't make this any harder for me than it has to be. I'm going to go meet the others before they have a chance to come here. Thank you, Taylor. When I finish whatever punishment they have for me, I'll come back to see you again."

I could tell. I could see in his eyes that he was lying to me. Of all the things for him to lie about, this is the one that I couldn't take. I couldn't just say nothing as he'd asked.

As I opened my mouth to speak, a knock came at the door.

16

We were all startled by the knock because it came at the most inopportune time a knock could possibly come.

"It's probably Father," Ferris said, rising to his feet.

Linus extended his arm out in front of him, blocking Ferris's way to the door. They made eye contact, and Linus just shook his head, making his way to the door instead.

When he opened it, Peter and Oscar were standing there.

"Wow, you've settled in quickly," Peter said, his tone filled with venom.

"Going to need the armor repaired. Stuff's junk. You trip on a rock and next thing you know it's flying apart," Linus said, laughing.

Oscar shook his head. "Enough. You need to come with us. Will you do it quietly?"

Linus just nodded, taking a step toward the door, but Peter put his hand on his chest and shoved him back a step. "She's coming too," he said, pointing at me.

"Why? I thought you just needed me to come. Is this an arrest or a party? Should we just go invite the whole village?" Linus asked, his tone coming across more desperate than mocking.

"Come on. You expect us to believe you'll behave? You will if she's with you, I'll bet."

Linus looked to Oscar but found no support from the quieter man either. "He has a point."

Linus glared at them both, looking between the two of them and me several times. He was trying to modify whatever plan he had on the fly, but it didn't look like he was coming up with anything. His breathing became deeper, and his jaw clenched. Now, he was only looking at the two of them.

"It's time to go, Linus," Oscar finally said. He stood aside, nodding for Linus to step through the door, then to me to follow them.

Ferris took a step forward, but Mother grabbed him by the arm, shaking her head. She looked just as worried and upset as him, but it was probably for the best that she stopped him. If Linus thought it was wise not to contradict them, it would have been an even worse idea for Ferris to try something.

When I stepped outside, Peter grabbed me roughly by the arm. "No running off, girl. Understand?"

I gritted my teeth and pulled against him, which I doubt he even realized.

Linus spoke for me. "She understands. Since you're making me do things this way, can we at least stop by Taylor's clinic so I can say goodbye?"

Peter and Oscar looked at one another, before Oscar nodded.

We walked for a few minutes in silence before finally arriving at the clinic and being greeted by Cara.

"Oh, hello, Taylor. I didn't think I'd see you today. Is…everything okay?" Her voice softened as she noticed Peter's hand holding my arm.

Linus walked over to our large animal cage and peered inside. The door was raised, and the lock was hanging loose.

"What happened here? I thought you had a camel in here yesterday. Does it look like someone tried to cut the bars in the back to you?"

We all tilted our heads almost simultaneously, and I started to step toward it to see what he was talking about, but Peter still held my arm.

"Do you mind?" I asked him, with a bit of bite in my voice.

He released his grip, and I leaned into the cage after Linus stepped back to let me through. I looked closely at the bars and didn't see anything out of the ordinary.

"Doesn't look like it to me. Not sure why someone would try to—" I felt a foot shove into my rear end, sending me falling into the cage. From my hands and knees, I spun my head around to see. It was Linus. He slammed the door of the cage down and fastened the lock. He took the key and handed it to Cara. "I'll kill you if you let her out before I'm gone. Understand, girl?"

Cara looked to me, then to Linus, clenching her fists and taking a step back. "I won't. I promise," she said, as she took the key with trembling hands.

"Linus, what are you doing?" I shouted.

"Things my way, Taylor. Not going to let them set the terms and use you some way to get to me."

"We weren't going—" Oscar started before Linus cut him off.

"Shut your mouth. You're a bigger snake than the one we just left dead in the desert."

"What snake? We don't know anything about—" Peter tried to speak, but Linus cut him off too.

"With all the noise we made? All of you know about it. Cut the crap. Let's go get it over with."

He walked away toward the gate only a couple of hundred feet from my clinic and stopped short of it, turning around and facing the two of them again. The three of them now had their sides facing me and barely within range of hearing.

"Why'd you stop?" Oscar asked. "I thought we were leaving."

"Saw Peter's hand hit the silent charge on his blaster. If you're that excited to kill me, at least look me in the eye when you do it. I didn't even think Peter was yellow enough to shoot an unarmed man in the back."

Peter rested his hand on his blaster. "Oh, come on, Oscar! He already knows we were sent here to kill him. Let's stop playing around. Whether the villagers know it or not doesn't make any difference."

"The commander didn't want us inciting the rebels...," Oscar said, his voice still calm and even.

"That doesn't even make sense. They'll be glad to see us killing one of our own. You can even stay out of it. We'll have us one of those high noon showdowns, and I'll show Linus here he's not the hot stuff he thinks he is."

"Peter...stop. She specifically asked you not to make a show of it. You're going to be reprimanded yourself at this rate."

"Let him," Linus said, tipping his hat toward Peter, then moving his poncho to the side to show the rifle.

"No! Please!" I pleaded, gripping the bars of the cage. "It was my fault. I asked him to come with me. I'm the one who should be punished!"

"It was within your rights as a villager to use the rifle assigned to your village to hunt the snake," Oscar said. "Linus, on the other hand, was forbidden to harm it, and this is just one of his many offenses. He's been given chance after chance. It was never going to end any other way."

I looked to Cara. "Cara, let me out, or I'll never forgive you!"

She hung her head. I hadn't noticed it, but she was crying, holding the key tight to her chest.

"Ready when you are," Linus said, nodding to Peter. "Better take a few steps to the side, Oscar."

"I won't. This isn't a game. Accept this with some dignity, Linus."

In a flash, Peter ripped his blaster from his holster but fired it before he could bring it up to aim properly, his head rocking back. His blaster let loose the shot that landed just in front of Linus, sending a spray of sand into his face. Peter fell backward onto the ground with a thud, causing a small cloud of dust to rise where he'd fallen. Dead before he hit the sand.

Oscar was only distracted a moment, his eyes wide as he looked down at his partner, but his hand was flying toward his own blaster even before he'd fully turned back to face Linus.

Linus had dropped to one knee, yanking the bolt back, slamming it forward to chamber a new round. Oscar drew his blaster and fired in the exact same moment, Linus fired his second shot. The blast had struck him in the side, sending him spinning and falling onto the ground. Oscar dropped his blaster and grabbed his neck with both hands, blood poured from between his fingers.

He dropped to his knees, choking out his final words. "You could've been a good soldier. You threw it all…away…," his last words came out garbled and quiet as he fell forward onto the ground. Linus dropped his rifle and tried to stand, blood pouring from the massive wound in his side. He took one step toward us but fell down onto his hands and knees. He rolled onto his back, coughing.

"Cara! Please!" I cried out, shaking the cage, tears pouring from my eyes.

She hesitated for a moment, then ran over and unlocked the cage. I ran as quickly as I could, stumbling and falling twice before I made it to where he was lying on the ground, holding his hand over his side.

"I'll take care of it! Let me see the wound," I demanded. "Cara, bring my medical bag. Hurry!" I shouted to her over my shoulder. She scrambled into the tent to retrieve it.

He just shook his head, refusing to move his hands. "Sorry, Taylor. I should've waited until we were out of the city and let them shoot me in the back, but I wanted to go on my own terms."

"Shut up. You're not *going* anywhere. After this, they're going to decide you're too good of a soldier to lose. They're going to punish you and make you go through some kind of training, and you'll be reassigned before you know it. *Move* your *hand*!"

Reluctantly, he agreed. When I saw it, I put both of my hands over my mouth, and all I could manage to do was tremble as I sobbed. I couldn't help him. No one could.

"H…hey," he said, his voice barely having any strength behind it now. "I was wrong."

"What do you mean? What were you wrong about?" I asked.

"Didn't think I'd ever be happy another day after I was recruited, but…you…being with you the last…," he paused, unable to continue speaking, taking a few deep breaths to try again. "Thank you, Taylor."

I grabbed his hand and held it tightly as I could. I wanted to say something in return. I knew I should, but I couldn't. I felt like I would choke if I tried to speak, and no words would come out. I lost myself again in my sobbing. I wanted to shout to the gathering crowd to help me, but I knew they couldn't. I wanted to scream at Peter and Oscar for what they'd done, but they were dead.

For a minute, Linus squeezed my hand in return, but his grip slowly loosened until soon there was no grip left at all. His eyes were open, gazing at the sky, but he wasn't there anymore. He was…gone.

I couldn't feel anything but the urge to scream. I wanted to beg him not to leave me.

A hand gripped my shoulder, and I didn't even wait to see who it was. I turned around and tackled them, landing blow after blow on their face, screaming with all the fury I'd been holding back.

It was Cara. She tried to shield her face. After a moment, I realized she just kept repeating the same thing over and over. "I'm sorry. I'm sorry. I'm sorry."

I jumped to my feet, shocked at the realization that I'd just attacked my friend. She was bleeding from her lip and nose and was still crying, making no effort to get up off the ground.

"Cara...I...," I clenched both my fists together in front of me, only now noticing they were both covered in blood, and screamed as loud as I could until I ran out of breath, and then I did it again. When I couldn't scream anymore, I grabbed the rifle, and I ran all the way out of the village as hard as I could, giving no thought to my direction or destination. I just wanted to run forever, until time ended, or until I couldn't feel the pain anymore, whichever came first, if either even came at all.

17

I ran until I realized where I'd been running and stopped when I arrived. I'd gone back to the snake, and I wasn't sure why. Maybe it was because it was the last place we'd gone to. Maybe it was guilt. Or, maybe, there was another reason.

I reached down to my side, relieved that I'd brought my canteen of water along. I drank everything that was left, which wasn't much, and fastened the empty canteen back to my belt. I sat on the sand and took in my surroundings. It was starting to get dark, but tonight would be a full moon— the only night where it was possible to see anything ten steps in front of you. Tonight, in particular, was looking to be a bright one. Just as visible as a cloudy day. It was still suicide to be out here this late, as that was when the most unkind inhabitants of the desert went out to hunt and scavenge, and I was sitting at an enormous dinner table with more than enough to eat for all.

Maybe I'd die out here, and they could have me too. I'd always cared deeply about the animals here, ever since I was a small child. I wouldn't blame them. After all, the unkindest animal of all was us, humans. No other animal would kill their own just for craving freedom. Suddenly, without the fear of death, I found myself craving the idea of going out with a bang myself, in a way. What fascinating animals might be drawn to the corpse of this snake? The biggest and strongest of the desert? For once, they wouldn't have to fight over their food, but they probably would anyway.

The vultures were the first to arrive. A few had even arrived ahead of me, but within an hour, there were more than I'd ever seen in one place. They paid me no mind as they crowded next to one another, eating their fill, but in such a hurry that one might wonder if they had somewhere they needed to be. Like some kind of family appointment that had been long planned and couldn't be missed and they were too afraid to pass up this once-in-a-lifetime opportunity. And, so, they ate as quickly as they could. I soon learned what all the hurry was about.

A group of boars moved in on the opposite side, but not before some of them charged the vultures, who had probably seen them nearby as they swooped in earlier. Guess I'd have eaten in a hurry too. The boar alone wasn't the most menacing thing in the desert, but the fact they traveled in groups and attacked anything that sought to compete with them made them a force to be reckoned with. Being that they only came out at night, like most animals of the desert, I'd only seen a few in my lifetime. In the wild, at least, not counting the domesticated ones in the village. I readied the rifle, just in case.

The next animal to arrive was an iron fox, but most villagers called them the gray fox. Their soft, gray fur and fluffy, white-tipped tails made them one of the most beautiful animals you could ever hope to lay eyes on in this inhospitable place. She approached cautiously, crouched low, moving only a few steps at a time, watching as the other animals ate aggressively. They paid no attention to her, and she intended to avoid them. One hit from a boar's long tusk, and she'd be dead, but that could be said of most animals. She settled in next to a small piece that had detached itself...well...that had been forcibly detached from the rest of the snake, away from all the other animals. She took small bites, and while she slowly chewed, she held up her head to survey.

It reminded me to stop watching them so closely and take a look around myself. The sands of the desert glittered in the moonlight since this light was far less overwhelming than the sun. I slowly laid flat onto the sand, looking up at the moon and stars. For the first time, I could finally feel some calmness returning to my body. I couldn't process everything that had happened today right now, even if I'd wanted to, and I didn't. I felt as though if I allowed all of the hurt to absorb into my mind at once, I would die or go mad. No one had come to be with me out here, and while I wanted to use that as yet another reason to hate, I knew that there was no way to follow me all this way. Why should anyone risk almost certain death to hunt down someone who clearly wanted to be alone?

A shadow passed in front of the moon and came as a welcomed distraction from my dark thoughts. But, what was it? Vultures didn't fly that high, certainly not that quickly, and no other birds that I knew of flew at night. Before I could spend too much time thinking about it, another distraction came. Just as fascinating.

A small herd of deer appeared over a dune and made their way over to the snake. The first to arrive bent down and pulled off a piece. I couldn't believe my eyes. Deer were previously herbivores, but ever since PanTech *sabotaged* our plant life, most of the deer had died and we couldn't afford to hunt them anymore. If we did, they might go extinct with no hope of ever returning. The ones that survived must have adapted to scavenge in addition to grazing on what little plant life remained. I had seen some eating cacti, but *this,* I hadn't expected. I caught myself desperately wishing Father were here. I wanted him to see this.

Father…what must he be going through right now? What if he was trying to fight through the crowd to get to me just before I ran away. I wanted so much to hug him and cry in his arms. I wanted to hear him tell me that I would be okay and that he and Mother loved me, and they would help me through it. But, Father wasn't here, and he hadn't been there either. It was a selfish thought anyway. Why would I wish that sight on anyone? Father had genuinely liked Linus, and already despised PanTech far more than I did. He might have tried to help him and gotten himself killed in the process…just as I'd wanted to do.

Linus knew. He knew that I would intervene to help him, and he'd taken us by the clinic because he'd remembered seeing the cage before. PanTech knew he cared for me, and they *used* me to hurt him. To catch him off guard and make him vulnerable, and to stop him from getting the jump on them. He knew exactly what would happen to him if he helped me hunt the snake. He knew why they were there. He helped me anyway, and I led him to his death. I may as well have shot him myself. Oh, Linus….

I curled up and began to sob again. Holding my hand over my mouth, trying not to be loud and disturb the animals nearby, but the fox had noticed me anyway. It stopped eating and was watching me curiously. It snapped its head around suddenly and bit something. A shadow passed over it, stopped for a moment, then attempted to fly away, but crash-landed a few feet away. The fox looked toward it and collapsed instantly…dead? Not a sound had been made. What was happening?

I changed my position to bending down on one knee, holding the rifle in my hand. Had I gone mad? It was like a ghost made of shadow. If the fox hadn't bitten down on it, or if I hadn't been watching her at the very moment it happened, I'd have never known for sure that what I was seeing was real. I still wasn't sure. Could she be sick? I crouched down as I walked slowly toward the fox. She was definitely dead if she let me get this close.

No...something was off. I leaned in closer, only to find that the fox was still breathing and breathing even harder as I got closer. Something moved again out of the corner of my eye, but by the time I focused on the spot, it was gone...if it had been anything. I gripped my rifle tightly. A small cluster of clouds was passing over now, making shadows jump and dance everywhere. One of the boars had started running in our direction, but before it could get too close, it fell flat onto the sand, collapsing midcharge. Was the flesh of the snake poisonous? Was it affecting the minds and bodies of these creatures to make them sick?

As the clouds cleared and the scenery was still again, illuminated by the full glory of the moonlight, I finally spotted something near the boar. It tried to take off but couldn't. Its wing was injured. It was smaller than the big vultures, but even if the vultures were the size of me, they couldn't have taken down an adult boar like that. Could it...? No.

But what if it was?

Impossible. I was still so upset. I was seeing things. I was going mad.

I rubbed my eyes and opened them again, but it was still there.

It might have been easier to convince me it was a ghost than what my eyes were showing me. This was a shadowfalcon.

Another boar charged after seeing his comrade collapse, and the falcon just barely made it out of the way. Why had it not paralyzed this boar too?

The boar charged again. This time the escape was even more narrow. The boar had bumped it through the air but missed goring it with its tusks.

No way I could miss this chance. Most people lived their entire lives without seeing one of them. No one had ever seen one up close. The few who had seen them were never believed, and here I was, nearly in reach of one, and about to stand there and watch it be gored to death by a boar? Not a chance.

I aimed the rifle, and just before the boar finished its third charge, I fired a shot that made it slide to a stop, making one attempt to return to its feet before falling again and going still.

The shot had spooked every animal around, sending a flurry of feathers into the air and boars charging in all different directions, though they didn't go far before slowly circling back. I approached the falcon, and he collapsed to the ground. He'd used their defense I'd heard about, which I had hoped wasn't true. It was said that a shadowfalcon would turn his paralysis weapon on himself and stop his own heart if he found himself cornered and unable to fight.

I walked over and picked up his body, my heart suddenly heavy again. I shouldn't have approached him like that. Then again, he'd have died anyway with his injury.

He was pitch black, and the glistening of his feathers wasn't too much unlike the starlight in the sky. His plumicorns were the only feathers on his body that weren't completely black, instead carrying a red tint. His eyes were a deep, solid green, and glowed eerily in the moonlight. Other animals with low light vision had similar eyes. His must be able to see through almost no light at all.

I sat him back on the ground and, with a heavy sigh, took a couple of steps back before something tugged at my gut. My instincts told me to look again. To look closer.

I picked him up again and realized that he was still alive, just barely. He must have used too much of his paralysis toxin against the fox and boar. Perhaps the fox's bite had startled him into using more than he realized. He had paralyzed himself completely, but his heart was still beating. If I brought him back home, I could treat his injury and heal his wing. I could come out one night and release him once he'd recovered. I needed this. I needed someone or something to need me the way this falcon needed me now.

I was going to save him.

"I'll call you…Ghost."

18

I wrapped Ghost tightly in my scarf, leaving only enough room for him to breathe, and wrapped a single wrap over his eyes so he wouldn't panic as much. I had planned to hunker down and ride out the night once I'd decided I even wanted to return at all, but by then, this animal would be in a full panic and would likely end itself once it built up enough toxin again. If he was to have any chance, I needed to return home immediately, and I needed the help of my only friend—a friend who I just screamed that I would never forgive and punched in the face several times.

This was a purpose I needed, and I needed to put it above everything else—even my own safety. If I couldn't give this shadowfalcon, what I once believed was a mythological creature, a chance, then I didn't want to go on living. I had to try at least to know I'd tried. To know I didn't let my lack of nerve and courage and weak guts stop me from doing the right thing.

Linus. Linus didn't let anyone or anything stop him from doing what he thought was right. He acted selflessly, even though he claimed otherwise, and spat in the face of death itself. There were surely so few men so heroic who ever lived before or would ever live after. I didn't care what beasts, hungry for fresh meat stalked me in the night. I would give them something, but it wouldn't be meat. It would be the fury I'd held inside me. That, I would give them, and they could choke on it.

I stood to my feet, cradling Ghost under one arm, my rifle under the other, and backing away from the approaching boars. One charged, and I quickly sat Ghost onto the ground next to me, aimed, and fired. It had to be the most stubborn and aggressive animal in the whole desert. Anything else would have been long gone by now. Another charged, and I had to shoot him three times. That's…two shots left. I think. What if Linus didn't get the chance to fully load it. I had no extra rounds on me. I could come back tomorrow with some men from the village, and we'd drag all of the boar back for slaughter, if there was anything left of them, but then they'd see the snake and panic. It would be best to let the desert take them. Plenty of hungry things out there would.

I picked up Ghost again and ran. The fox still wasn't stirring, nor was the boar he'd paralyzed, so he would probably be like this for a while. I had no way of knowing for how long. The fox was a beautiful creature in its own right, and I felt a pang of guilt for not being able to take her too. I would return if I could, even though it would almost certainly be too late for her. She was probably already dead.

Cloud cover came again, and I could no longer see where I was going. Before it became completely dark, I crouched down next to a large rock and tried to focus on what I could hear. A lot of good it would probably do me, but it was all I could do. The desert was full of silent killers. Half of the things in the desert could kill you without making a sound. Some, like Ghost, could kill you without *you* even making a sound.

There was nothing but silence, occasionally interrupted by a gentle breeze. A normally gentle breeze, at night, in the desert, was anything but gentle. With everything that had happened, I didn't even have time to stop and realize how cold I was even though I was freezing. It wasn't dangerous, but it was extremely uncomfortable. Yet another reason few people ventured out at night, and no one went into the open desert like this. Was my family worried for me? Did they assume I might be already dead? Would Cara care, after what I did to her?

Oh no, what if my father and brother went out looking for me. Normally in that situation, they would request to use the village's rifle. But I had it now. No, not now. I couldn't get caught up in all of this now. I'd start thinking about Linus again, and….

I felt something shift my clothing and crawl over my leg. A snake, or maybe a lizard, or scorpion? I stood completely still, only shifting my eyes so that I could see the light returning as the clouds slowly blew past. The light came agonizingly slow as I felt whatever it was crawl even further up my leg.

When the light finally came, I found myself wishing it was any of those three things I'd considered. Even all of them. It was a terror ant. I couldn't see the nest, but I wasn't covered, so this one must've been the scout, trying to figure out what to make of me. I resisted the urge to leap to my feet and flee. I had to be patient. It would eventually crawl away from me, but the moment it did, I would have to leave. If it suspected I was edible, it would send a scent back to the nest, and I'd be swarmed.

Just as it crawled off of me, darkness came again with more clouds, but I couldn't risk staying. I would rather die by the teeth, claws, tusks, or stingers of almost anything else in the desert than to be eaten alive by terror ants. So, I ran, in total darkness, in the direction of the village. I still wasn't close. I was miles away. The snake had been near the boundary, and I was less than halfway back.

Two bullets left, with one chambered and ready to fire. I still had my knife, too.

Running in the darkness was basically begging to be killed, and any number of creatures might give chase and kill something strange that obviously couldn't see where it was going as well as they could.

Ghost still hadn't stirred, so I at least had that going for me. My legs burned, and my lungs ached. I was still battered from the fight with the snake and fighting to get out of that cage. My body had all but given out on me as a reward. I couldn't allow it to. I pushed hard and found myself agonizing over the thought that the empty canteen bouncing around on my belt would offer me no relief. The cold air that filled my lungs, which was so much different from the comforting warmth I was used to, did no favors for me either.

The light was just up ahead, moving slowly to meet me across the sand, the friend I needed right now, offering me the only chance I had of making it back home alive. Once I made it a few steps in, I continued running but strained my neck to look over my shoulder, ready for anything.

Nothing was there, and it seemed that, at least for this brief moment, I had a little luck left in me after all. I slowed my pace to allow my legs a chance to make a slight recovery.

I was able to walk like this for a while. It was quiet. Too quiet. I could see Linus's face again and hear his last words. He told me I made him happy. It felt strange because I also wondered if I would ever be happy again. We'd only known each other for a few days, but I'd never felt that way about anyone before. My mood swung wildly from sadness back to anger again when I thought of the life we might've had together. The children we might have had. Grandchildren. I *hated* PanTech for taking him away from me. They *would* pay for this.

A movement far away caught my attention. It was a panther. They were strictly nocturnal and normally shied away from humans, but that was during the day. At night, I must have looked just as delicious as any other animal caught out alone, away from the rest of its herd. It walked with legs sharply bent, taking long and careful strides. I continued with my pace more or less the same. I didn't want to run, or I knew it would immediately give chase.

I'd hoped that our uneasy truce would hold, at least long enough for me to get close to the lights of the village. It would run away then, surely. But, those lights weren't in sight, and I was about to lose what little light I did have, as another inopportune cloud approached. I had seconds, and I couldn't take the chance.

I stopped, sat Ghost on the ground, and fired a shot at the panther. It jumped just as I'd raised the rifle, causing me to miss. Of all the times to miss....

It ran toward me, full power and speed, and I aimed as carefully as possible. One shot left. Just one shot. I drew in a deep breath and held it, steadying myself as much as I could, but it wasn't enough. There's just something about a black panther charging at you against a fading light, with your last shot that does something to the nerves. I fired again and missed. This was it.

No! I still had my knife, and I drew it. I still had my fingers. I'd stab it until the blade broke and gouge its eyes if I had to. I still had life in me, and as long as I had the life to breathe, I had the life to fight. I threw my rifle at it as it was about to pounce and screamed, hoping against hope that it would be startled at an unusual sound from its prey it didn't normally hunt. It wasn't. I was knocked to the ground hard, and I felt claws dig deep into my shoulders. Before it could sink its teeth into my neck, I was able to plant my knife all the way up to the hilt somewhere into its body. I'd hoped the neck. The other paw slammed into my other shoulder, not digging in as deeply, but enough that I lost grip on my knife. I slapped and clawed at the beast's face as it tried to maneuver to deliver the killing blow.

Light was coming from somewhere now, but I couldn't look away from the panther, or I was dead. After a short moment, the light was bright enough to make out the features of its face. The beast cried out and jumped backward. As it did, I saw a spear sticking out of its side, which the wielder quickly pulled back. I couldn't make out the figure. The lantern was placed on the ground, at their back, and they were only a shadow. Female, I thought, but I couldn't say for sure.

Had Cara come to rescue me?

The figure held the spear in a warrior's stance as the panther charged again. She thrust it into the beast's leg, took two steps forward with incredible finesse, and threw two more thrusts into the panther's chest before it could jump back.

Was that...?

"Mother!" I shouted.

"Run, Taylor. I'll stop it from following," she said, with surprising calmness.

"Not until I find Ghost! He's here. I just put him on the ground."

She brought the spear in closer and held it above her head, leaning forward—some kind of exotic stance I'd never seen before. The panther ran but soon turned back around. They fought this way. If they were wounded, they'd run a few steps away and turn to use their charge, and did this repeatedly. Their endurance was greater than anything else in the desert—even the boar's.

"Take your time. This will be over soon, and I'll help you look."

Still calm, with a voice as even as stone. First, she knew about the PanTech armor, and now she fights with more skill than almost any man I'd seen. I had so many questions, but between what had happened with Linus and now finding and rescuing Ghost, there just wasn't room in my mind.

Just as I found him and the rifle, the panther charged Mother and pounced through the air. She stood straight, then stepped to her left, as though it were part of a dance she'd performed thousands of times, spinning the spear in an arc and slicing it across the side of the panther's neck. It must have realized the fight was not in its favor anymore because it turned immediately and ran away, off into the direction it had originally come from.

I took a step forward but fell to my knee. My body had reached its limits.

Mother ran over and caught me before I fell. "Mother, listen…this…shadowfalcon. Find Cara. Tell her to bring the small animal cage. Don't unwrap it."

I spilled all of this onto her because I thought I would pass out, but somehow I didn't.

Mother slipped my arm over her shoulder and helped me walk. We walked, and walked, and walked, but neither of us could find words for the other. At times, I would catch her looking down at me, with the saddest expression on her face. All of my mental power was invested into screaming at my legs to keep walking. One more step, then one more, until finally we'd reached the village.

Every inch of my body protested and seemed to threaten me if I chose anything other than immediate medical attention and sleep, but that's not the choice I had to make.

I glanced down at Ghost. Still calm, for now. I had to go to Cara and say whatever was needed to make her forgive me. We had a mythical beast to save.

19

As we entered the village, I could feel my strength returning. At least, the illusion of strength. I had not slept, and it was nearly morning. It would be early morning for Cara when I woke her. She was nearly my age but lived alone. Her mother had died when she was very young, and her father died just a couple of years ago. She'd be more than capable of taking care of herself, but I worried for her, and I imagined she must feel very lonely.

Especially with a friend who punches her in the face....

"It's alright, Mother," I said, weakly. "I can make it to Cara's from here."

I held the rifle up toward her, but she shook her head.

"I know you. You'll bleed out trying to save that bird or wait too long to clean your wound. I'm better at cleaning and sewing wounds than you might think."

Normally, I would've been skeptical of her statement, given how pretty and delicate Mother went out of her way to be, but now...now, I wasn't sure. There was more to Mother than I realized, and for some reason, she'd kept it from me. Soon, I'd push for an explanation, even if she didn't want to give one to me. But soon felt like it was so far away. For now, I trusted her.

"I believe you," I said. "But...you don't have to. I'm sure Cara can check my wounds while I get started on Ghost."

"Ghost...I can't believe you've actually captured a shadowfalcon, Taylor. I've never seen one. Your father swore he'd seen one, as a boy, but I'd always wondered if he was mistaken."

"Mother?" I asked, after a moment of silence.

"Yes?"

"What did they do with Linus?"

She took a deep breath and let it out slowly. "Your father and your brother insisted on burying him in the village graveyard. I tried, but I couldn't talk them out of it. I spoke to the other two PanTech employees that came by later to retrieve them and told them we were planning to bury the other two next so it wouldn't look suspicious that we'd only buried Linus. They accepted my explanation, but still took the other two back with them. And shortly after," she sighed, "they returned to take Linus's body as well. I'm so sorry, Taylor."

I slowly shook my head. "No...he's gone. It doesn't matter if his meat and bones are here, or there, or wherever. They took him away from me either way...."

Mother leaned her head down and touched it to mine. We stayed that way for a moment. It caused my tears to flow again, but I sealed them off no sooner than they'd started.

"Come on," I said. "We need to move quickly."

A moment later, we were knocking on Cara's door. She opened it up almost immediately. So quickly that it startled me. When she saw it was me, she took a step back and hung her head.

"Taylor...I'm—"

"No. *I'm* sorry, Cara. Sorry for everything. I'm sorry for the things I said to you earlier. I'm sorry for hitting you. I'm sorry too for strolling into your house in the dark hours of the morning, bleeding on your floor, and with an injured animal that needs saving. Will you please help me?" I asked, tearing up yet again.

Pull it together, Taylor. You don't have time for this.

"You didn't need to ask," she said. "Tell me what you need and…wait. Is that…?"

"A shadowfalcon? Yes."

Cara put her hand over her heart, taking a step forward to get a closer look. "This is a sign from the gods, Taylor. It must be. I don't know what it means, but it means something."

"Maybe, but the gods aren't here to patch him up. Mother's going to tend to my wounds while you assist me, so I won't be moving. I need you to take me to a clean table and fetch my bag from the clinic. Bring a sheet of leather, about half an arm's length, and one of our smaller cages. I have some thick long leather gloves there as well. You know the ones. I'd been working on them to use for handling terror ant hives. I'll need them to handle him once his paralysis wears off."

She nodded with each thing I mentioned. "Got it. Anything else?"

I knew there'd be a lot of things I'd forget. Poor Cara would have to do a lot of running.

"Some water for her, please," Mother added.

Cara nodded, then motioned for us to follow her. She led us into a room with a large workbench and items made of leather hanging all around: belts, gloves, aprons, and more.

"I didn't know you did leather-working," I said.

"I do. I'd love to talk about it now, but I know there isn't time. If there's nothing else, I'm off."

I nodded. "Thank you."

I turned and leaned the rifle against the wall before laying Ghost across the clean workbench. I unwrapped my scarf from his body but leaving it over his eyes and began looking him over. Now, under the light of a brighter lantern, he looked even more amazing. But better than that, he looked alive. Completely immobilized by his own toxin, but still breathing shallow breaths. I gently extended one wing, the wing I already suspected of being healthy and studied it as a reference. I expected his other wing to be broken when I slowly, *very* slowly, extended it but was relieved to see that it wasn't.

At the same time, my mother had pulled back my shirt to check my wound. Her sigh gave away that it was a little more serious than she was hoping, but not life-threatening— just a lot of work.

I was somewhat embarrassed, but I knew I would have to take my shirt off so my mother could treat the wounds. That's just the way it would have to be. I attempted to raise my arms above my head but found that I couldn't.

"It's alright. I'll cut them off. They're destroyed anyway," Mother said, sensing my frustration at the thought of having my arms forced above my head, then potentially having to do delicate work on a shadowfalcon.

I nodded.

"Alright. Do it."

She picked up a pair of shears from one of the shelves and began cutting. I shut it out of my mind. I wouldn't let it distract me from the task at hand.

"I'm sure Cara has extra clothes for you after we finish and you're all bandaged up."

"As long as you can do it while I'm working, do whatever you need to do."

"You're going to work at the same time?" she asked.

"I don't know if it can wait that long. Just be as gentle as possible, but do what you have to do. I can take it, I promise."

I only hoped that I wasn't lying, but I needed her to believe that I knew it for a fact.

She pulled out her first aid pouch, and I recognized it as the one from earlier that she was going to use on Linus. Conscious thoughts of him started creeping back into my mind. His hand squeezing mine. His last words. The way PanTech had killed him on the street like he wasn't the great man he was. I'm glad he killed them both. I wish I could have killed them myself.

"Taylor? Are you alright?" Mother asked, noticing that I had drifted off into my own thoughts.

"No, Mother. I—"

Cara interrupted me as she burst back into the room. She immediately turned her back after seeing me. "Oh, sorry! Should I...?"

"No, Cara. Just be thankful we're not outside at the clinic or even in the tent. Put my tools on the end of the table, and fetch me some cactus wine. Mother will need it, and so will I."

Cara said nothing, just followed my instructions, placed my tools next to me, and ran out of the room. She returned quickly with the wine. Mother poured it carefully over my wounds before handing it to me. I attempted to turn it up, as I desperately wanted a drink, and thought it might help me with my nerves and a bit of the pain.

Mother put her hand under it and helped me bring it to my lips. I drank several big gulps and sat it on the table before nodding to Mother.

"I'm ready when you are," I said.

She positioned herself to my right, and Cara stood to my left. I examined his right wing carefully and found several feathers had been crushed. Unfortunately, he was bleeding from all three of them. A bird didn't have much blood to lose.

"No break—" I winced as the needle entered my shoulder. I clenched my teeth and did my best to speak through the pain. "No breaks on the…ah…wing bones, but three feathers are…ow…broken, and they are blo—" I drew in a sharp breath. Thankfully, Mother was ignoring my obvious distress, just as I'd asked her to. "They're blood feathers. I need pliers, and starch, quickly."

Cara ran out of the room, quickly returned with the starch in a small bowl, and grabbed a pair of pliers from a drawer. She grabbed the bottle of wine from the table and poured some onto the pliers, wiping them down with a clean cloth, then handing them to me. I plucked the three feathers rapidly, then reached for the wine from Cara. I nearly dropped it when Mother pulled the stitching tight and cut it.

"See, I'm even faster than you," she teased.

"Probably because I'm not as rough," I said, almost allowing myself to smile. I poured wine onto the wounds, then picked up some of the starch and stuffed it onto them. "With those feathers out, the bleeding can stop. He was—" I winced as Mother poured wine over the smaller wound on my other shoulder. "He was lucky," I finished.

"So were you by the look of it. What happened, Taylor?"

Mother had begun expertly wrapping my bandages as we spoke.

"The long story will have to wait. The short story is that the desert is a hard place to survive at night," I replied. A thought struck me. "Oh, the fox! There was a fox that was still there too. Got hit with Ghost's paralysis toxin. We need to go…in…the morning."

At first, I thought the floor in the room was rising but realized that when Mother grabbed one arm, and Cara the other, it was the other way around.

"I'll take Cara. If it's still there and alive, we can handle it. You need to rest," Mother insisted.

I sighed. "No, I…," I didn't even bother finishing that sentence. I wasn't kidding anyone. There's no way I'd be able to go out at first light, which was probably coming very soon, to check on the fox. It would be selfish of me to insist that I be the one who goes. Cara *could* handle it, and if Mother could handle herself that well at night, alone in the desert, she could certainly handle the mostly gentle creatures that roamed the desert by day. "Okay," I conceded. "You win."

"Good, so I'll cage Ghost and make sure the bandage around his eyes is tied well, and you won't need anything else."

"Hey Cara," I said.

"No, Taylor. I'm not hearing anything else from you. You're going to lie down and rest."

"That's fine but…could you at least get me a shirt?"

"Oh!" she said, wincing. "Sorry. Of course."

"And…thank you," I added. "Thank you both."

20

My dream was familiar. I was lying on my back in the sand, and my skin felt comforted by its soft bed of warmth. The sun kissed my face like a loving parent and made me feel safe. A gentle breeze passed over me, giving me goosebumps and making my skin tingle in the most wonderful way. A figure approached in the distance. I could hear it screaming, but I couldn't make out what it was saying or who it was. It bent down over me and continued whatever it was doing, but I was undisturbed. A small herd of deer walked past, and I tilted my head ever so slightly to watch them attentively. They weren't scrawny like the ones I'd seen reluctantly chewing on the remains of the snake. Their coats were beautiful, and their eyes were sharp. One stopped to look back at me, chewing a mouthful of grass, as calm and at peace as I was. If I weren't so comfortable, I'd have gone out to see it. I wasn't sure how, but I knew it wouldn't flee from me; we were too content to leave what we were doing.

The figure over me was still yelling, and I could start to hear it now, almost like a whisper. "Move your hand," it seemed to say. That's what it was, a little louder this time. "Move your hand," she shouted. It was a woman, but who? She kept repeating the same thing. "Move your hand. Move your hand. Move your hand!"

My hand. My hand? I looked down, and I was holding both hands over my side. I was wearing armor, like what PanTech soldiers wear. When I saw my hands, my feeling started to change from serene comfort to agony, unlike anything I'd felt before.

"Move your hand!" she shouted again.

Finally, I listened and moved my hands. The wound was grotesque. Was I dying? Of course, I was dying. Nothing would survive a wound like this.

The girl grabbed my hand and held it tightly, her body shaking with sobs. I could almost make her out, but not quite. Her voice was certainly familiar. Very familiar. Was that…?

I could feel my body going cold, slipping into that eternal sleep we all eventually fall into. I could feel my grip loosening on her hand, but she only gripped tighter. At least I could make out all of the features of her face as the last of my strength slipped away. It was…me.

I sat up abruptly as my sleep broke, and as bad as the physical pain in my body was from having moved that quickly with my shoulders freshly wounded, the agony of sadness I felt was so much worse. At that moment, the desire to die again filled my mind and my heart. I wanted it more than anything. To die and be free of the pain. If the gods were real, and I saw Linus again, all the better.

"Glad to see you're awake, but would you mind moving a little slower. It always hurts worse the next day, so you better preserve the stitches that are in there now," Mother said.

I tried to laugh, but even though I could normally fake a laugh in any situation, all of my will couldn't summon one now. Instead, I started crying again.

"Oh, Taylor…," she said, leaning toward me. "You dreamed about Linus, didn't you? I'm sorry…."

In an instant, the switch flipped on my emotions, as they often did, and I growled with the surge of anger. "Don't be,"

I said, slowly lowering myself back onto the bed. I noticed something odd out of the corner of my eye. Was that...?

"Is that the fox sitting on your lap?" I asked, craning my neck to see better.

She continued stroking the fox's fur and smiled. "It is. Isn't she beautiful?"

I nodded. "She is but...is she still paralyzed?"

Mother sighed. "Completely. I've been watching both her and Ghost. Not so much as a twitch yet."

"If they don't come around soon, I'll have to force water into her. Ghost is too small for that, and he'll need to start eating soon so he can heal properly. I should have asked you to—"

"Get some of the boar meat? Oh, we did. I've saved some to feed Ghost and the fox, but we're going to have some fine meals at home too."

"Mother...?"

"Yes?" she asked, tilting her head.

"How do you know how to dress a boar, track a person through the desert night, and fight a panther off with a spear? And, how did you know about Linus's armor? The way it was supposed to come apart."

She grinned. "That's a lot of questions all at once."

"You don't have to answer them in any particular order, but could you answer them?"

She looked away, stopped stroking the fox for a moment, and seemed to contemplate on the request. "I don't like talking about it, but...you deserve an answer."

I said nothing, suddenly filling with the anxiety of thinking I knew at least some of the answers already.

"I was born in a different adversity zone. There, it was much larger than our village. It was a kingdom, and the ruler of that kingdom was called Emperor."

I held up my hand. "I'm sorry. Just…give me a moment to process that. You weren't born here? You must be the only one here who wasn't. How is that even possible?"

She smiled, but it was a pained smile. "I'll get to that part. It'll be easier if I just explain as I go."

I nodded.

"When I was a small girl, things weren't so bad for the people of the kingdom. However, when I was fifteen, the old emperor passed away, leaving his young son to rule the kingdom. Most things stayed the same at first, but it wasn't long before the differences started to reveal themselves.

"The new emperor was obsessed with surrounding himself with young, beautiful women. They worked in his palace, dressed him, prepared his meals, and even served as his private bodyguards. One day, I was out in the fields with my father, tending to our farm, when the emperor walked by with his new bodyguards. I marveled at them at first. They were so beautiful but fierce at the same time. I caught his eye, and he called for us to speak with him.

"I never saw my family again after that day, and I still don't know what happened to them. It wasn't until after I was forced to join the emperor's service that I recognized the sadness in most of those girls' eyes and came to know it well."

She sighed, dabbing her eyes with her sleeve.

"You don't have to keep going if you don't want," I offered, suddenly feeling remorse for how harshly I'd judged my Mother throughout my life. It seemed I knew very little about her.

"No. It's alright. It's been a while since I spoke about this, is all," she collected herself and continued. "At first, I was a dancer. Being so young, I wasn't much good for anything else. I quickly realized that the girls who didn't put much effort into capturing the emperor's attention were placed in the most difficult roles. I was moved to the position of assisting one of the palace's doctors after failing to capture the emperor's eyes anymore as one of his dancers.

"But, after noticing the emperor rubbed his shoulder often, I borrowed a recipe from one of the doctor's books for a salve to soothe muscle pain. I convinced the emperor to allow me to apply it and give him a massage, and before long, I tended to him daily. On my nineteenth birthday, I was moved to his personal guard and trained with the spear."

"Wait," I interrupted. "Did you decline to join PanTech after taking the exam?"

She shook her head. "The emperor had much power, but he thought he had more than he did. Every year when it was time for testing, he would hide away all the young women and forbade them from revealing themselves or taking the exam. It wasn't until I was twenty-three that PanTech soldiers marched into the palace. The emperor ordered his bodyguards to protect him, but none dared. He was dragged away screaming, and I don't know what they did with him after that.

"PanTech installed a poor young woman as the new empress, but I'm not sure what came of that. A large exam was held to accommodate all the women who had been denied in the years previous. I passed, was more than happy to leave, and was assigned to the role of soldier. As a soldier, you can leave that service young. It's actually one of the most sought-after positions in PanTech, and anyone given the role must be both exceptionally bright and physically able. I completed many years of service and met your father shortly before my time was up. Since he'd declined his invitation to join PanTech, despite his exceptional score, I made up my mind to stay here with him."

"I didn't know soldiers could do that. That means Linus really could have stayed here. I could have declined my invitation if I passed the exam. And...," I trailed off, choking back the urge to cry again.

"I'm sorry, Taylor. I wish I could've done something to stop it."

"Why did you keep this from me for all of these years? Even Father didn't tell us, and Ferris doesn't seem to know either."

"He doesn't."

"But, why?" I asked, pressing.

"I was asked not to," she said.

"Just like that?"

"Just like that. I know you don't like PanTech, but my experience with them was different than yours. They were my savior from a far worse situation. If you must be a slave, better to serve the more righteous master than the cruel one."

"Yeah, I'm not so sure I buy into that, Mother. Sorry."

"I understand. I don't expect you to. You're your own woman."

"Do you? Do you really understand? Because it sounds like you don't. I'm sorry your life was awful, but when you and Father fell in love, you were able to be together. Linus is *dead*. We can never be together now. He died because he helped me and because he saved our village from that giant snake you saw. You did see it, right?"

She sat quietly for a moment, considering everything I'd said with far more calmness than I'd expected. "So that's why they went after him. But…that shouldn't be worthy of execution, and how did they know so quickly?"

"They heard me shooting, I'm sure."

"Yes, but not him. All we heard in the village was your rifle firing, not his."

"I don't know, and I don't really feel like going to ask them at the moment. It was probably a newer tracking technology on their armor or their blasters."

"I don't think—"

As she began to speak, the fox raised her head, and we both froze to watch. No sooner than she had done so, she lowered her head again.

"The paralysis must be wearing off. That means Ghost will be moving soon if he isn't already."

"It's alright. Cara is in there with him. She came home just before you woke up. She wanted you to come and see her when you came to. She has something to show you."

21

I walked into Cara's shop, closing the door behind me, and found her working on something at the table. Ghost stood up in his cage, eyeing everything with caution and curiosity but a distinct lack of fear.

"What have you tied around his legs?" I asked.

She brightened up. "So glad you asked. This should help you control him a bit on your glove. Your glove, I reinforced with two additional layers of leather, by the way."

I scrunched my chin and nodded repeatedly. "I'm…really impressed, actually. I had no idea you could do all this. What's that you're working on now?" I pointed to the leather piece she'd stretched over a wooden ball in front of her.

"Oh, this?" She held it up and spun it in her hand. "You know how birds don't really pay attention to things they can't see? I thought this would help you train him if you had him around other people."

I held up my hands. "Oh no. Absolutely not. I am *not* taking him out around other people. The hood is a good idea, but he's staying a secret for as long as I can keep it."

Cara frowned. "Why not? Ghost will give everyone hope. It's a good omen, Taylor."

"Let's say that's true. All the more reason to keep him a secret. If PanTech finds out that everyone thinks he's some kind of good omen, a sign of prosperity to come, they'll pluck him right in front of everyone. We have to maintain an optimal level of adversity, remember?"

"Okay, if you say so. You're probably right anyway." She frowned, and her shoulders sagged, but she continued stitching.

"Sorry to be so depressing, Cara. And…sorry for what I did to you. You didn't deserve—"

Cara shook her head. "No. You don't need to apologize. I'm sorry for what you went through. I can't even imagine what you must've felt, so please don't apologize to me."

I smiled and wrapped my arms around her shoulders. "Thank you, Cara. I was worried you might not forgive me."

"Oh, please," she said, playfully, returning to her stitching. She looked from the hood to Ghost, then to the hood again. "You know, maybe let's let him get more used to us before we try to put this on."

"That would probably be a good idea," I said. "Say…I wonder why the toxin doesn't immediately kill what it comes into contact with. It seems to be potent. From what I could tell, it runs from some kind of glands above his beak, onto his beak, and enters the bloodstream when he slices something with it."

She shrugged. "Maybe he measures the dosage somehow?"

"Sure, but he doesn't inject it directly, like a snake. He basically drips it onto the open wound. Then there's the rumor that they're able to turn the venom on themselves to kill themselves if they have no way to escape imminent death. Obviously, swallowing it doesn't have the same effect, or they'd accidentally contaminate themselves with it all the time. It must be some kind of backward path into their own bloodstream."

Cara sat the hood down, scratching her chin and leaning back into her chair, staring at Ghost intently.

"Too bad we can't just ask him," she said.

"Hey, Ghost. We're really curious. Would you mind explaining your toxin to us?" I asked.

Ghost looked between the two of us as though he were genuinely trying to understand the sounds we were making. Maybe he was.

She sighed but smiled. "Okay, obviously we *can* ask him. Thanks for that."

"You're welcome," I retorted, my tone much brighter than it had been. I really was thankful for Cara. We were never competitive the way many girls were, despite our closeness in age and our working together. Cara always put her relationships above any kind of recognition. She preferred to live quietly and stay out of the way, attracting as little attention to herself as possible.

It's what I wanted, too, or so I thought. Either I was lying to myself, or I was just really bad at it.

A knock came at Cara's door, and a muffled voice carried over the other side. "Your brother and Father are here, Taylor, and I could also use some advice on what to do with this fox. It's alert and looking around."

Cara and I nodded at one another, and she put a small sheet over Ghost's cage before we exited the room.

Father and Ferris were both gawking at the fox when we entered the common room as Mother continued holding her. Ferris started to reach out and touch it but stopped when he noticed that Cara and I walk into the room.

"Taylor!" Ferris yelled, making the fox recoil. "You're awake."

I held my finger over my lips and pointed to the fox with my other hand. "It's a wild animal, Ferris. Please don't scare it. And, yes, I'm awake."

He and Father stepped over to me and wrapped their arms around me tightly. Too tightly, and I winced. "Do you mind?"

"Yes, do you mind?" Mother echoed. "I've already scolded her about minding her stitches, and I told the two of you only a few minutes ago."

The two of them abruptly released their hug at Mother's scolding, and Father laid his hand lightly on my shoulder. "I'm sorry, Tay. I'm sorry I wasn't there. I would've tried to help."

"Then I'm glad you weren't, and I'm sure Linus would've felt the same way. He stopped me from helping him, and he'd have found a way to stop you too. Only PanTech is to blame for this, and no one else."

The silence in the room, which extended far longer than it should've, gave away the agreement. Even Mother didn't argue with me this time, although I was sure she didn't quite feel the same way. She was a retired PanTech soldier, after all.

"Anyway...," I continued. "I have something to show you, assuming Mother hasn't ruined the surprise."

Mother beamed. "Oh no, I wouldn't dare," she said, handing the fox over to Cara, who had been standing there with her arms open, hinting that she'd like to put it away. "Just remember," she said, looking between Ferris and Father. "I was the first person who got to see it after Taylor."

"Everyone, follow me," I said, making my way back into Cara's room, leaving the door swung open behind me, allowing everyone to funnel in. "Stay at that end of the room, please," I added, looking over my shoulder as I approached the cage.

I slowly pulled the sheet from the cage, revealing a suddenly alert but seemingly fearless Ghost.

Father and Ferris stood there for a moment, frozen, and silent. Ferris leaned forward as though he was trying to stretch just a little closer to make sense of what he clearly didn't believe he was seeing.

Father dropped to his knees. "Oh, gods. I can't believe it. I always knew they were real. I saw one when I was a boy, but no one believed me. No one has ever captured one. Not as long as this village has stood. Not even PanTech has managed it. Taylor, you are...," he hesitated. "I'm sorry to say this, considering the timing, and circumstances, but you are blessed by the gods to have performed such a feat. This must be an omen, but I don't know what kind."

I'd never heard Father mention the gods so directly before. It was highly frowned upon to discuss them anymore, and Mother and Father never did all that often, even behind closed doors. Her, I could understand. They weren't her gods, after all, but I was fairly certain Father didn't even believe in them. I was even more certain that I didn't. If they existed, they clearly had less power than PanTech.

"PanTech doesn't care about the gods, Father, and the gods don't care about PanTech. He will be kept a secret so he doesn't end up plucked and cooked in the town square. If I hear one more thing about how he's an omen, I'm going to lose my mind. He's a bird, albeit a rare one, but *just* a bird. Maybe I should have named him Omen instead of Ghost."

Cara shrugged and smiled.

Father rose to his feet. "Sorry. I was just a little overwhelmed. When I was a boy, many more people talked about the shadowfalcon than they do now. Some even said that the one who could tame the bird would be the chosen of the gods. I had even heard that the gods would grant them immortality."

I shuddered. "Sounds like a curse to me."

"Then you should probably stop behaving as though you're immortal, then," he said, shaking his head. "I just still can't believe it. A real shadowfalcon…, have you noticed how closely he pays attention to us? He looks between us as we're speaking. Did you notice that? Do you…?" he hesitated for a moment but continued. "Do you think he understands us?"

Despite the urge to dismiss it, I had to consider this seriously. "I have noticed, but I'm not sure. I don't think he understands us now. How could he? But maybe he is actually trying to. It's possible that he's studying our tone and our actions when we say certain words, like a small child learning their parents' language. Or, maybe he's just curious, as most birds are, and we fascinate him. He's probably seen just as few humans as we've seen of his kind. I just expected him to be more…more—"

"Afraid?" Cara interrupted. "I expected him to be terrified. That's why I rushed to make him the hood, but now I'm not sure he'll even need it. Do you think there's something wrong with him?"

I shook my head. "No. I think bravery and stupidity may just be his blessing and curse. He reminds me of…well…Linus." I paused for a moment, not daring to continue speaking, feeling the tears welling up in my eyes and my voice choking. I closed my eyes and looked down for a long moment. "I'm going to take good care of him."

"*We're* going to take good care of him. I'll be with you every step of the way. Whenever you need help treating him, or if you need your glove repaired or new accessories for his training, just come to me, and I'll help you," Cara said, smiling.

I took a step toward Cara, my arms extended out, and embraced her in the tightest hug I could muster. It hurt *so* much, but I didn't care. I didn't deserve a friend like Cara. I'm not sure anyone did.

Mother stepped up beside us and put her arms around us both. "We're all here for you, Taylor. I don't care what PanTech says. You've had enough adversity for a lifetime."

I lost my battle with the tears, and they flowed freely from my eyes. I tried to answer but couldn't even choke out anything resembling words. I released Cara and hugged Mother just as tightly. She stroked my hair as she held me gently in her arms. I never knew for certain if she loved me, and I always doubted that she did, but between the previous night when she saved me in the desert and the way she held me at this moment, I knew for certain that she loved me so much. Everything she'd ever said or done was to help me because she knew that beauty, charm, and manipulation were weapons, just like the spear or sword. She wanted me to be able to use them effectively. I should have listened to her.

Finally, I was able to slow the tears enough to compose myself.

"I love you, Mother."

Father and Ferris stepped over and joined in our growing group hug, and I couldn't help but notice the oddly curious expression in the falcon's vibrant green eyes.

22

Unfortunately, I had no idea what I was doing when it came to training a falcon. Luckily, I had foundational knowledge that gave me a great place to start. I understood birds, but Ghost was no mere bird. In days, he was able to follow verbal commands. Days. Not weeks. Cara has been there with me for the first couple of nights, far out into the desert. She had to fetch leather to strengthen the glove on that first night after Ghost's talons went right through it. The end result ended up being three times as thick as before and a stiffer leather. Ghost didn't seem to mind. Then again, he didn't seem to mind anything.

Unless Ghost was just an oddity, even amongst other shadowfalcons, I found it difficult to believe that there were many of these creatures out there actively avoiding humans. Ghost had several chances to leave. On the third night, I cut the leather strap bindings from his legs, half expecting him to flee. It would have been alright with me if he had. I never liked the idea of *owning* an animal like this and keeping them against their will with no chance of escape. Yet, when I cut the bindings, he appeared completely uninterested. Did he lack the intelligence to realize that they were gone, or was he actually choosing to stay? It was surely the latter, but...why?

It went on like this for several more days. On the sixth day, I killed a rabbit, showed it to Ghost, and in hours he'd gone out and retrieved another rabbit. Dead, like the one I'd shown him.

"How do I tell you to bring it back paralyzed and not dead?" I asked.

Ghost tilted his head, first to one side, then to the other.

"Can you understand me? Are you...trying to learn to understand my language?"

A restrained chuckle came from behind me.

"What are the two of you talking about over here?" Mother asked, petting the fox she was holding in her arms.

Now that Cara had finished modifying the glove, she didn't need to come along with me every night. Mother volunteered to come instead and insisted on bringing that iron fox with her. I was sure they'd end up killing one another, but they didn't. Somehow.

"Ghost is trying to tell me something. Or, nothing. I can't figure him out. When I speak to him directly, he tilts his head. Have you noticed that?"

"Omen does that too, you know. Maybe they're just curious," she said, shrugging.

"Omen? You named her Omen? Seriously? I know you've taken to her, but I really wish you'd left her home."

"Hold on. One criticism at a time, please. Omen and I were just out taking a walk. Do you own the desert now?" she turned her head away from me in mock frustration, punctuated with an exaggerated *hmph*.

"No. Do you?" I asked.

"Not everything holds a grudge like you, Taylor. Ghost barely even notices her."

"And what about Omen?" I snapped. "She's nervous. Look at her ears pulled back and her tail tucked."

"And why do you think I brought her? Like all of us, she will need to face her fears quickly. Otherwise, she will lack confidence and be vulnerable forever. In this, we and animals are alike," she said.

"That's because we *are* animals, Mother. Also, how did she become friendly with you so quickly? You've handled foxes before, where you're from, am I right?"

Mother smiled and nodded, scratching Omen's neck before putting her down and watching her run off into the vastness of the desert. She smiled again, pulling two wooden swords from her belt.

"Why don't you send Ghost to fetch a rabbit? Since I can't reason with you to stay out of trouble, I should teach you to be better prepared for it."

I hummed a deep tone, and Ghost flew off.

"Nonverbal commands. Clever," Mother said, tapping her chin and smiling, tossing me a wooden sword with her other hand.

I let it fly past me and land on the ground. "You're letting her go?"

"She deserves to be free. She isn't like Ghost, Taylor. She's more like you. She'll never listen to anyone. She'll only be happy going her own way."

"But…she seemed to really like you," I said.

She laughed and sat down on the sand, patting the spot beside her.

I sat down next to her and rested my head on her shoulder.

"Taylor. If it's alright with you, could you tell me about Linus?"

I looked up at her, surprised. I wanted to be upset, but I couldn't find the emotion.

She seemed to notice my expression.

"You don't have to. It's just that you were never really interested in boys these past few years. Your father and I wondered if you would ever be. Your brother talks about a different girl every day, it seems. You always seemed to hate PanTech so much, and he was a soldier. I know there must be more to him than I realized. We could see how you'd fallen for him. I just want to know more about him."

I stared down at the sand for a long time, hugging my knees to my chest. Mother deserved to know more about him.

"Linus was…," I began, but my voice caught, and I found myself unable to fight back the tears.

Mother wrapped her arm around me and hugged me tightly. "It's alright. You can tell me when you're ready."

"I'm…," I sniffed and took several deep breaths. "No, I'm alright. I just need a minute."

She nodded and kept her arm around me tightly while I considered how to put it into words. Did I even know what made Linus so wonderful? I hadn't thought about it in terms that could be explained. I just…felt it.

"Linus was brave. He was bold, and somehow he put everyone else before himself and also followed his own path. No matter what the consequences were, he did what he thought was right. He went against his fellow soldiers, his commander, and even PanTech itself, and it didn't even matter to him if he won. All that mattered to him is that it was what he wanted to do, and he thought it was the right thing to do. I've never met a man like that before. It only took a few short days before I really knew him. The way he stood up to the chieftain for that girl he didn't even know, and for me. The way he went with me to fight the snake…it was my responsibility, not his. This was my village, not his. These are my friends, my family, and neighbors, not his. He did it for no other reason than because it was the right thing to do. I knew when we'd killed the snake, and he protected me from the explosion, that I loved him with all my heart. Maybe he didn't feel that way about me, not yet, but I…just knew. If we only had time…."

I lost my composure and the battle with my tears. Mother hugged me tightly.

"I knew the same with your father, Taylor. The day I met him, I asked him to show me his inventions, days before PanTech decided to destroy them. He hated me at first. He was convinced that I'd asked about his inventions as a spy and reported him. It was weeks before he would speak to me again. In the end, he found that he loved me more than he hated PanTech, and I loved him more than I loved PanTech. I'm so sorry, Taylor. I wish you could have had the same chance. It's unfair that was robbed from you. I know it doesn't seem like it now, but eventually, you will heal, and maybe you'll find another, worthy of your love."

"I know what you're saying is true, Mother, but right now it—"

I was interrupted by something suddenly appearing in front of us, slamming onto the ground. I squeaked and fell backward, and even Mother jumped a bit.

In the dim lantern light, I could see that it was a rabbit, but I was also pretty certain of the fact that they don't just fall from the sky.

"Ghost, was that you? Ghost, get down here! Bad Ghost!"

Mother held her hand over her mouth in a failed attempt to hide the growing snicker.

I put my hand on my chest and took a deep breath, then let it out. "He nearly frightened me to death. I didn't teach him to do that."

"Maybe you were right," she said once she finally managed to stop laughing.

I shook my fist at Ghost...wherever he was. "About what?" I asked.

"About him being clever. I believe he was playing with you, startling you for a bit of fun."

No way. Could he...? No. "He probably just dropped it by mistake."

Ghost suddenly appeared in front of us, landing on the ground near the rabbit, and looked up at me. He nodded toward the rabbit.

"You...want to eat it?" I asked.

He nodded toward it again several times.

"Okay. Eat it."

He walked over to the rabbit and began eating it, more slowly than I expected.

"Did you see that, Mother?"

"Do you still think he's just a mere bird?" she asked.

"I don't know what to think. What about you?"

She shrugged. "You're the expert, Taylor. Your father believes he's nearly divine, perhaps more than nearly. Cara seems to believe the same. You are in a better position than anyone else to learn the truth."

"The truth scares me sometimes," I said.

That might be the truest thing I'd ever said to Mother, except it was more than just the truth that scared me. Maybe that's why I tried so hard to appear like I was scared of absolutely nothing. Maybe I'd convinced everyone of that. Now I just needed to convince myself.

"Me too, Taylor. I think the same is true for everyone, except for maybe your father. But, enough of that. Since Ghost will be busy for a bit longer, I'll train you with the sword tonight. On one condition."

I raised my brow. "Oh? And what might that be?"

She grinned. "You have to let me teach you how to apply eye makeup."

I rolled my eyes. "Fine. Deal."

She smiled, and I felt a warmth come over me, like walking up to a fire on a cold night. This feeling was followed quickly by a sting of guilt, remembering all the times I'd disrespected Mother, and assumed she had the worst of motives that she didn't love me. That she only cared about herself and being pretty. Or that she might faint at the sight of dirt on her clothing. Although I wouldn't dare allow her to know it, I now very much looked forward to putting on makeup together.

"Wise choice," she said. "Today, it will be the sword, and tomorrow we will go over a few hand-to-hand techniques. Go ahead. Pick it up."

I leaned down and picked up the wooden sword, doing my best to copy her stance.

"Ready?" she asked.

"Ready."

23

The next month went by like a blur. I continued taking Ghost out at night for training and sleeping in a couple of extra hours in the morning. I'd moved him into my room, and he'd healed up nicely. It was still much safer to have another person with me, just in case I was accidentally hit with his paralysis toxin. Not to mention his talons were sharper than any knife or spear I'd ever seen. Even though he'd never tried to hurt me on purpose, I still had to be extremely careful.

Ghost's rate of learning was nothing short of incredible. In only a few weeks, he'd gone from staying on my arm without being held, to flying back, to chasing a lure we'd made from rabbit fur, to going out and retrieving rabbits of his own and bringing them back. Now, he'd mastered attack commands and differentiated between commands to use his toxin, or not use it, and whether or not to kill. Sometimes, when I'd let Ghost hunt for a while, Mother would continue teaching me sword technique and hand-to-hand combat.

Still, she preferred to instruct me as she always had, in the arts of charm, persuasion, and beauty. Only now, I wasn't so dismissive and rebellious. Although I didn't choose to exercise these skills...well...*ever* really, I still committed them to memory, for a time when they might be practical and useful. I'd taken to wearing my hair in dreadlocks, the way Father had when I was younger. Mother helped since my hair was much different from his. To my great surprise, she approved of this new look. She said it added a layer to my unusual beauty. In reality, I valued the extra few minutes of sleep it bought me, and although I did enjoy the look, it really was more about saving time. Sacrificing beauty for a few minutes of rest, now *that* Mother probably wouldn't approve of. Then again, she did scold me for not getting enough sleep because she claimed it would cause me to get bags under my eyes. There were only so many things I could juggle at once.

My eighteenth birthday came, and Father gifted me one of his smoking pipes. The one Linus smoked the day before he…was murdered by PanTech. Despite Father's encouragement, I wasn't ready to smoke it, even though I valued it greatly. Cara had given me a pair of leather boots she'd made with the help of the village's cobbler. Mother had given me a strange black dress. She said it was one of her most prized possessions and that it was her only thing left from her home. She'd worn it when she left to join PanTech. It had ridiculously baggy sleeves and an equally ridiculously wide belt that wrapped around the waist. I thought it looked embarrassingly silly, but I didn't dare say such a thing to Mother. I accepted it with great appreciation. If nothing else, because of how much it meant to Mother. That alone made it mean something to me.

It was now only a matter of weeks until the exams started, and I would have to decide if I passed, whether or not to join PanTech and leave the village. I was leaning very strongly toward staying and continuing to run the clinic. Mother and Ferris felt very strongly that I could make a bigger difference if I joined. Maybe I could work my way up in the hierarchy after a while and change how things were run. I think I'd always believed shadowfalcons were more likely to be real than the possibility PanTech could be changed from the inside. Then again, shadowfalcons *did* turn out to be real, so I couldn't exactly dismiss that based solely on the odds of it happening. I just didn't know if I wanted to be the one to waste my life on a long shot like that. I'd be just as happy, probably happier, running the clinic for the rest of my life and personally passing it on to someone else. Or was I just lying to myself?

One week after my birthday, Cara invited me to her home. She said there was someone I should meet but left out any other details. When I arrived, a young woman was sitting at the table with Cara. She looked older than us, probably in her late twenties, and wore a warm smile that didn't seem to weaken upon my arrival.

"You must be Taylor," she said, her smile still unwavering.

I returned her smile, cautiously. "I don't know who you must be," I admitted.

"Taylor, this is Lucille," Cara offered. "She's a friend of mine, and I thought you might like to meet her. She's someone who hates PanTech just as much as you do."

I nodded but immediately felt nervous. I had a feeling I knew where this was going, but I was put in the awkward position of neither being able to say so aloud nor knowing what I'd say even when I could. "Nice to meet you, Lucille."

"Taylor, I promise I'll get to the point quickly, and I won't waste your time. I know you're a busy woman, and you were probably preparing for your exams coming up since you just turned eighteen."

I shook my head. "Not exactly. I'm thinking I'm going to refuse admission if I pass."

"Is that because you like it here or because you hate PanTech?" she asked, leaning forward, resting her elbows on the table. She was still smiling, but with a small adjustment, it took on a more mischievous feel.

"Both. After all, my father stayed, but PanTech stopped him from pursuing his work because it would reduce the adversity of children in the village. Thankfully, they don't care so much about animals. As long as the animals aren't benefitting us, I'm free to help as many as I want. My teacher actually failed the exam but was a pretty decent veterinarian anyway."

Still smiling, she shook her head. "You forgot the part about PanTech."

"I'm sorry, but I don't really want to talk about PanTech. I despise them. They took someone important away from me, and I'll never forgive them for it. Don't bring them up again, or I'm leaving." My breathing hastened, and my blood started to boil. It was an all too familiar feeling over the past month, as I struggled to keep my already bad temper, now much worse, under enough control to function from day to day.

She held up her hands in defeat, finally letting her smile fade from her face. "Not even if I offer you a chance to harm them, right here in your very own village?"

My skin tingled, and my anger gave way to knots in my stomach. "You're a rebel. One of those that PanTech is staying outside the village to collect information on."

"And yet, we're still here. Not one of us has been caught, and we've stayed one step ahead of them at every turn. We know we can't take them in a fire fight. Our sticks, and rocks, and spears are no match for their rifles and blasters. We don't have special suits to make us stronger, faster, and stabilize our wounds. We don't have vehicles to cover distant land in minutes or limitless wealth from PanTech to replenish anything lost or damaged. What we do have, is the human mind. In this, we are the same. No different at all. What we can do, Taylor, is outsmart them and outmaneuver them."

I stared at her for a moment, locking eyes, and after that moment, I was sure she'd look away. She didn't. Her smile didn't return, and she remained stoic and confident. This wasn't a pitch. This was the truth. At least, the truth as she understood it, which is all the truth is to any of us. I broke the connection first.

"Cara, why did you invite me here to meet Lucille? Are you...?" I started but thought better of finishing the question.

"No. I'm far too scared to be a rebel, Taylor. You know that. But you...you're brave. You're so smart and so brave, and most importantly, you have—"

I shook my head subtly, and fortunately, Lucille wasn't looking in my direction when I did. Don't you *dare* mention Ghost. Cara took the hint.

She continued, without doing anything to acknowledge my gesture or missing a step. "—such a kind heart."

"I'm sorry, but I'm not sure kind hearts is what a rebellion needs. I better—"

"It's not the kind heart I'm questioning, Taylor," Lucille interrupted. "It's the 'brave' part."

She eyed me up and down. I wasn't about to take the bait. "If you say so. I think I'd better go."

Lucille continued on as though I'd said nothing. "Between your pretty mother and the renowned genius of your father, I don't think you've had a truly hard day in your life."

"Uh-huh," I said, standing up. "Good evening."

"The only PanTech soldier you'll ever hurt is the blonde one you got killed."

I had only begun to turn to leave but whirled back around, took a step toward the table, and jumped into the air, stretching out my body in a drop-kicking motion aimed for Lucille's face. She slid her head to the side and wrapped her arm around my legs, pivoting and throwing me off into the floor.

I jumped to my feet as she reached for my shirt, grabbing her wrists and twisting them as best I could to throw her off balance, using her forward momentum against her, just the way Mother had shown me. It worked, sending her tripping to the floor, scraping her chin, and bloodying her nose as she landed face first while I held her wrists to prevent her from breaking her own fall. I twisted her arm behind her back, and without even realizing what I was doing, I put her in a position to dislocate her shoulder.

Before I could pull back to finish the motion, Cara grabbed me and began pulling me away.

"Taylor, stop! Please. She's just testing you," Cara said, as though that would make a difference.

"I know she's testing me, but...," I turned my attention to Lucille. "If you *ever* speak of Linus again, if you so much as whisper his name, I will *kill* you!" I shouted.

Cara put her fingers to her lips, desperate for me to lower my voice. "Shh...someone might hear."

Lucille rolled onto her back, finally finished with her moaning from what must have been an extremely painful impact to the nose. "Hah! I wasn't expecting that at all. I think I learned my lesson today. Maybe it's time to retire that tactic since I can't back it up anymore. She's right that I was testing you, and you passed."

I pulled against Cara, growling as I dragged her with me toward Lucille, ready to finish what I started.

Lucille threw up her hands, surrendering. "Wait! Before you jump on top of me and start bashing my face in, ask yourself which you hate worse: The lie I told to make you angry, that you were the one who got him killed or the people who *actually* killed him."

I stopped, feeling the motivation to fight fading from my muscles. That question was easy to answer, and it was easier to answer than I realized. If the rebels had a way to hurt PanTech, I wanted a piece of that. Maybe for every bit of pain I gave them, it would heal a part of the pain they gave me. Not that we could ever be even. It would never be enough. Even I knew that, as consumed by it as I was. But that didn't stop me from making the decision.

I didn't answer the question, only offering a question of my own. "I'd like to meet the rest of you. How soon can you introduce me?"

24

It turned out there was going to be a meeting tonight, and Lucille invited me along. I was blindfolded and led through the village. I couldn't tell which house we entered, but I knew we were still in the village and that we'd entered a house. After walking through the house, a door opened, and I stepped down into a passageway where we continued walking straight for some time. Was this a tunnel? It must've been, and building a tunnel beneath the sand is no easy task. No wonder PanTech hadn't been able to find them yet. A hiding place this elaborate wasn't something they were likely to expect.

Eventually, we opened another door, and I heard several people stop talking as we entered the room. Lucille removed my blindfold, and four other people were in the room with us. Lighting was dim, and everyone sat close around a small table, with only a small candle in the middle.

"I guess it went better than you thought, huh?" a small woman said, looking to Lucille.

Lucille shrugged off the comment. "Everyone, I'd like you to meet Taylor. Taylor, meet Heather, Ludo, Lapis, and Cairn. Ludo is our leader. He and his father discovered this natural cave and turned it into what it is today."

I'm not sure what I was expecting. An army? Uniforms? PanTech soldiers held prisoner in dungeons? We were a small village. A large group would've been discovered already. I should've realized this earlier. Only a small group like this could possibly operate underneath PanTech without being discovered by now. It was stupid of me to think any different.

Ludo was a large man who must've been in his late twenties. He was easily among the biggest men I'd seen and, unlike the others, wasn't someone you'd forget if you'd seen him before. I had, of course, seen him many times. He was the cobbler Cara worked with to create the boots I was currently wearing. As though reading my mind, he spoke up in his deep voice.

"How are those boots working for you?" he asked.

"They're exceptional. I didn't think of you as a rebel type," I said, not keen on allowing the change of subject to go any further.

Lapis, a brown-haired, round-cheeked older woman, laughed. "So much for the small talk."

Ludo grinned. "What is a rebel type, Taylor?"

My mind immediately went to Linus. He was not so much a rebel but a hero; in a world where the bad guys are the ones with the power, the hero has no choice but to rebel. Someone who always has a problem following orders or believing what they're told. Someone who didn't have a problem being mean to people who were mean, and hurting people who hurt people. That's what I imagined when I thought of a rebel, but now that image only brought me pain. I wanted to say all those things aloud. Instead, I said nothing.

"Taylor?" He leaned forward, trying to get a closer look at me under the dim light that made it difficult to make out anything but the most basic of features.

I shook my head. "There's no such thing, I guess. I don't seem like a rebel type either, I bet. But, here we are because someone has to be."

Cairn, the oldest one there, spoke up. His long, graying hair was the most visible of anyone's, reflecting the candle's tiny dancing flame. "I couldn't have said it better myself."

Lucille's smile was back in full force. "Are you kidding? You say that yourself all the time."

That got at least a chuckle out of everyone—everyone except myself and Ludo.

Ludo motioned toward a chair for me to sit in, which I did. "It's probably about time we got down to business. Don't worry about something as trivial as joining a group, Taylor. If you want to help, we'll be happy to have your help. And if that help is hurting PanTech, then we're on the same team."

Everyone nodded solemnly at that.

He continued. "PanTech brings in supplies to trade with the village at least once a month. This time they brought extra, probably because of the extended stay that was planned, thanks to our little club here. Looks to be about three times as much, which does a couple of things. One, it gives us an idea of how long they plan to stay before resupplying. Two, it makes things a lot more difficult for them to keep up with, given they have the same number of soldiers as always. With three of them down, now there are only four left. It's hard to even have a rotating sleep schedule with that many soldiers. It's even harder to waste time guarding medicine, and food, and wine. We're going to sneak in, and with a simple distraction, we'll walk out with a fortune. That is, as long as the distraction can keep going for more than a few minutes."

I spoke up. "What's the distraction?"

He stared at me for a moment before answering. "Well, you just had to ask the one thing I hadn't thought out yet."

I looked down, considering whether or not I should offer up my own idea on the matter.

"You have an idea, don't you?" he asked, reading my mind yet again.

"I'll go into the camp and ask to speak to the commander. I have a lot to say to her, and it'll be interesting to the other soldiers there. I was with the three soldiers who died, and I can give her a recounting of the events that took place that no one else can. She'll listen to me, and I'm sure she'll have plenty to say. While she's speaking to me, the rest of you can sneak in to carry out as many supplies as you can before she and I finish speaking."

Ludo shook his head. "You do know she'll kill you if she realizes we're taking the supplies? That woman is as sharp as a tack, and she has an enhancement. That means she can break your neck before you realize she has her hands on it. No, we should come up with something—"

"Come up with something different if you want," I interrupted. "It's something I'm going to do anyway, so you may as well take advantage of the opportunity. Or, don't. It's up to you."

Ludo smiled. "Well, what can I say to that? I guess that plugs the hole we had, then."

Lapis shook her head. "Maybe, but is this really the kind of mission we should be bringing...well...is it really a good *first* mission?"

Cairn laughed. "*First* mission? This is the first *real* mission for any of us. PanTech doesn't exactly leave a lot of openings. We've been waiting years for a chance. She's just as ready as any of us are."

Ludo nodded several times, clearly wanting to move the conversation along. "You're both right, and she's just as capable as anyone here, from what I understand. Lucille wouldn't have brought her here otherwise, and I trust Lucille's judgment.

"Now, onto the plan of action. We are going to take a wide trip around, and the same wide trip back. We'll leave several minutes earlier than Taylor, both to avoid suspicion and also to make sure we get there just a little after she does. Cairn and I will take a look at the map tonight.

"We'll have to be quiet, which means no carts near the camp. We'll bring them with us, but they'll have to be left a good distance away to make sure they're neither heard nor spotted."

"So, how are we supposed to get anything of value if we have to make big, long trips to our carts?" Heather asked.

Ludo shrugged. "That's a limitation we have to live with, Heather. We can move quickly, but we just have to move quietly."

"Sure," she argued, "but wouldn't we be better off not bringing carts at all since they'd just slow us down, and we're probably only going to get one trip in without putting Taylor at risk anyway?"

Ludo opened his mouth to speak but stopped, and everyone sat quietly for a moment.

"She has a point," Cairn said. "Carts are going to slow us down a lot on the return trip too. If anything at all happens, we'll have to abandon them."

Ludo nodded. "Yes, probably for the best that we just go with packs and just fill up on whatever we can carry. Focus on the smaller, more valuable items. Less likely they're going to notice anything missing that way too. I doubt they pay much attention to inventory if they even keep inventory at all since nothing is ever missing."

Lucille slapped the table. "Here's a crazy idea. You ready?"

Everyone looked at her, but judging by the tired expressions on their faces, they already knew and didn't like where this was going.

She continued. "There's only four of them. We can bring our weapons, ambush them, and steal their armor and blasters. We'd have plenty of time to take the supplies, and if the suits let us leave the boundary, we can go and look for other zones to join us using their vehicle to cover a lot of distance we normally couldn't. When the next group comes in to relieve them or see what's wrong, we ambush them with our new weapons and armor, and repeat the process, maybe even with help from other zones. We could be the first step in a long march that leads all the way to headquarters."

Everyone looked back and forth between one another as a cloud of dread seemed to descend on the room. I liked the plan, personally. There are only a few problems.

"I like it, but it won't work," I said.

Lucille shot me a glare, and for a moment, I thought she might take a swing at me. "Because of the commander's enhancement? If we get the jump on her, it won't come into play. Once she's out of the way, the other three will hardly be a threat at all if we're careful."

I tapped my finger on the table, shaking my head. "That's not the problem…or at least, *maybe* that's not the problem. I don't know much about the commander, other than the fact they all see her as unbeatable. Maybe she isn't. The problem is with just about everything else. The suits can't just be taken off and put on anyone. They have to install them into the person at headquarters, and they wear them all the time. They're attached to the soldier's body. They're filled with fluid that has to be changed. They're really complicated. We'd need to study them for a long time, and even then, we wouldn't have the technology to fit them onto someone else or replace the fluid.

"Then there's the blasters. I've never seen any soldier fire another soldier's weapon. What if they're somehow unique to them too, and only that soldier can use them? Then, there's the boundary. We have no idea what allows them to go through it. It might have nothing to do with the armor. Maybe they have some kind of key put into their bodies that allows them to walk through no matter what. That's something else we'd have to study, and even if we did find some kind of key embedded into their body, there's no guarantee we'll be able to use it.

"If even one of these things goes wrong, which is almost a guarantee, the plan is going to end with all of us getting killed. Possibly the moment we attack the commander."

Lucille sighed and slammed her fist onto the table. She didn't try to argue or ask any questions. She just leaned back in her chair, seething.

"One step at a time," Ludo said. "Let's keep an eye out while we're there and see if we can learn anything new. It seems like our biggest disadvantages are always the things we don't know. Get a good night's rest. Tomorrow, for once,

PanTech will get as good as they give. Let them experience some adversity for once."

25

The next day, we employed our plan. I took the straight path to the PanTech camp, and the others took a wide, semicircle approach. They might've thought it bold or clever for me to come up with this distraction so quickly, but the truth was much less complex than that. I wanted to meet the commander. I wanted to see if she was open to clearing Linus's name or telling me more about him. I wanted to know if she was as terrible and scary as everyone made her out to be. Even though the truth was less complex, it was probably just as stupid. It took being curious about terror ants and digging them up to see if everything you heard about them was true.

Still, something about the commander just seemed...off. She didn't behave like a professional soldier. She was more like Linus than the others, but none of that made sense. Is that why she gave him so many chances, or did they not get along, and that's why she wanted him dead? Was he competition? Probably not, since Linus hated being a soldier. He'd never try to make commander rank. But then again, did PanTech really care what anyone wanted for themselves? When it came down to it, I just didn't expect the commander to kill me. Maybe she'd threaten me or punish me in some way, but she didn't seem to care enough.

As I approached the gate, I noticed there weren't any soldiers standing out front this time. Not wanting to startle anyone, I whistled loudly. For a few minutes, no one came. Was the camp abandoned? Did they assume that if they left it unattended, that no one would be stupid enough to walk in and take the risk? Normally, that might be a fair assumption, but they knew about the rebels. It's why they were here. Was this a trap? Did they know about this plan somehow?

I whistled again, louder this time, and shouted "hello" as loudly as I could. Again, I waited, and no one came. I fought the temptation to just walk in…for now, at least. I had to be patient. Ludo and the others may have arrived ahead of me and gotten caught. No, that shouldn't happen. We went over the pacing thoroughly. They should still be several minutes away. So, what was taking so long? I whistled a third time, and this time two soldiers came to the gate.

"State your business!" the first shouted.

Before I could answer, the second soldier spoke up. "Wait, isn't that the girl from before? The one who came to see Linus?"

"It's me," I shouted back. "Can I come closer, so we don't have to yell?"

They looked between each other for a moment before the first soldier waved me over.

I approached slowly and stopped a respectable distance away. From where I stood, I could tell that the second soldier was a woman, due to the feminine shape of her armor, which was in stark contrast with her deep voice.

"Would it be possible for me to meet with your commander?" I asked, with all the faux confidence I could muster.

"Absolutely not," the female soldier snapped. "No one can just walk in here and meet with the commander, or any of us really. The only reason you were able to meet Linus is because he wanted to meet with you. We have rules to follow and protocols to observe."

"That's right," the male soldier agreed. "Besides, we don't have time to babysit you, considering we aren't even getting breaks now, thanks to that free-for-all."

The female soldier jabbed him with her elbow. I guess this wasn't something they were supposed to admit so freely.

"Irrelevant," the female soldier said. "You should be on your way before—"

A figure stepped out of the tent behind them, revealing the beautiful, fire-haired commander.

"Oh, what's this all about?" she said, her voice overflowing with amusement.

"Ma'am!" Both soldiers shouted, spun around, and saluted in perfect unison.

"This girl—" the female soldier started.

"I wasn't asking you," she said. "I'm asking her." She pointed at me.

"I…uh, wanted to meet with you," I stammered, caught off guard by her sudden appearance and forwardness, though I shouldn't have been.

"I don't know. I like visitors as much as anyone, but that didn't work out so well for Linus, now did it?"

My cheeks flared with heat at the sudden wave of embarrassment. They really were somewhat alike, but she didn't stumble over her words the way Linus did with that kind of remark. She was quick and knew precisely what to say to throw everyone off their thoughts. She would not be easy to speak to. This was a mistake, but one too late to take back.

"I…no. I just wanted to speak with you about Linus. Would that be alright?"

She sighed and held open the tent door behind her, waving me in.

I stepped inside and tried to absorb as much of my surroundings as possible.

Tables lined the outer edges of the tent, each dedicated to a different task. Suit parts lay strewn across the longest of them, to my right. I recognized them. They belonged to Linus, Oscar, and Peter. Several pieces were damaged beyond repair, but what would I know? I'm sure PanTech has the knowledge and means to repair things I couldn't even comprehend, or reduce the pieces down to their base materials to build new armor, the way a blacksmith would melt iron and forge a new tool. Too many questions flooded my mind, but I wouldn't waste time on trivial things. I had little enough of it that it was precious, and I had to choose every question carefully.

A large tank sat in the corner with hoses attached. Was this the machine that cycled the fluid in their armor, or was it used for something else? Since it sat near the pieces of armor, I suspected it was the former. Blasters and rifles rested on the table that ran along the back of the tent. There's not much mystery there beyond the obvious ones. Along the left side table, there appeared to be several small sealed containers in boxes. Food and drinks? It couldn't be ammunition. Their guns didn't use it. Medicine?

She pointed to a chair in front of the table in the center, and I took a seat. A fourth soldier stepped into the tent, walking to the corner, only stopping for a moment to regard me. All wore their helmets except the commander, so I couldn't determine anything about their appearance beyond the bulky, dull, gray armor they wore. The soldier, who I assumed to be male based on their armor's appearance, nodded to the commander and walked into the corner, attaching one of the hoses to his armor. It seemed I'd guessed correctly. This was the machine that recycled the fluid used in their armor. It took every ounce of my willpower not to ask about it.

Four of them were in this tent. The commander was now sitting in front of me, two behind me guarding the tent's exit, and now the fourth doing maintenance on his armor. This was a good fortune I didn't expect to have, and I wasn't about to squander it. Play it smart. Play it carefully. *This is your moment, Taylor.*

"So, you aren't here to make friends, which is a shame. Just business, then?"

"What? No...I mean, yes. I wanted to talk to you about Linus."

"Right, Linus," she said, frowning. "What about him?"

"Why did you order Oscar and Peter to kill him?" I accused flatly, doing everything I could to mask the rising anger and prevent it from spilling into my voice even as I asked the question.

"That's a lie. Who told you that?" Her playful expression faded immediately, and she looked every bit as angry as I felt. Except, she made no effort to hide hers.

"Oscar and Peter said it. I heard them myself."

"I told them they were authorized to use force *only* if Linus attacked them first."

"Sounds like an obvious loophole. They tricked him into shooting first, so they could kill him. I'm *glad* they died in the process. Human garbage," I said, gripping my hands together tightly in my lap. So much for containing my temper.

She narrowed her eyes at me. "Are you calling me an idiot, girl?"

I stood up from my chair, sending it toppling over behind me. I heard both guards behind me unholster and charge their blasters, but I didn't look back at them. "I do! What kind of fool gives an order like that, knowing they already hated each other?"

She stood up and flipped the table to the side, leaving nothing but open space between us. It was done with so little effort, so little movement, that it might have been a sheet of paper or a blade of grass, yet it must've weighed hundreds of pounds.

I stood my ground, my fists clenched, not unaware of the surge of fear that left me mostly paralyzed. I could feel tears building up around my eyes, but I wasn't about to stand down.

She stomped more than stepped and stopped directly in front of me. She brought her hand down toward my face but stopped abruptly, running her fingers through my hair instead with a mischievous grin. For a moment, I couldn't believe what was happening. I couldn't move. I held my breath and thought I might faint. When at last I finally regained control of my body, I pushed myself away from her. I drew back my hand and tried to slap her with all the force I could muster, but in a blur that was impossible for my eyes to follow, she caught my hand. I stared at her grip in disbelief, but when I looked at her face, she was still smiling.

"I love it when someone has the guts to talk to me that way. So exciting. It's what I liked about Linus, too. It can be so boring around here, you know." As she let go of my hand, she pushed me back, sending me falling to the ground. "You got what you came for. Linus was wrongfully murdered by his fellow soldiers. I'll amend the report and clear his name."

"T-thank you," I stammered. "May I go now?"

She laughed and shook her head. "It's my turn. I have some questions of my own, so listen closely."

I nodded, trying not to show my fear, but by now, I'm sure it was written all over my body.

She continued. "Your village has a bit of a rebel problem, as you know. Do you know them?"

I shook my head.

She laughed again, louder this time. "You're lying. I can tell. Doesn't matter, though. I want you to be my informant. My pretty little bird that flies in and listens to the important details then flaps her way back to me to sing the whole song. They'll talk to one of their own. Will you do it?"

"N-no!" I said, probably more surprised at my own words than she was.

"Fair enough. How rude of me. Let me make you an offer. I'm one of the few in PanTech who can order a physical enhancer, like the one I'm fitted with, when I deem it necessary. How would you like to have one? Don't answer. Let me sweeten the deal even more. You're a veterinarian, so assuming you pass your exam, I'll let you bring a species of your choice back to study. Surely that appeals to your scientific mind. This is an opportunity rarer than you realize, but you see, I'm fairly lazy as an adversity zone manager, and I prefer to just let things run themselves. You could save me a lot of work. You scratch my back, and I'll scratch yours. What do you say?

I opened my mouth, but my throat caught. Ghost. I could bring Ghost with me, but what was I thinking? I wanted to destroy PanTech, regardless of whether she was telling the truth about Linus or not.

"You still hesitate? Fine, think about it. The offer stands until you refuse it, so I'll advise you not to rush. Go on; you're free to go." She nodded to the soldiers standing behind me, who I'd forgotten about. "Escort this pretty little firebrand out of my camp."

The soldier who had been standing in the corner the entire time remained stoic. I could only imagine the expression they must be wearing on their faces. Oh, how I hated those helmets.

I gritted my teeth as both soldiers came up behind me and grabbed an arm each. I didn't dare fight them. I'd already gotten far too lucky. She was every bit as dangerous and unpredictable as I thought she'd be, but not quite as cruel, somehow.

I walked quietly with the two soldiers to the exit of the camp, where I was assisted with a generous shove that sent me toppling to my knees. That had taken a while, for sure, but I was playing with fire. More than I could likely handle, but that wasn't what mattered at the moment.

They had plenty of time to grab all the supplies they could carry.

My work here was done, and then some.

26

It turned out Ludo and the others were able to get their hands on a lot of supplies and were probably gone long before the commander and I finished our conversation. Food, medicine, clean water, cloth, leather, iron, and more. Ludo promised they'd begin distributing the supplies to the people of the village in need of them as soon as possible, and I felt good that I was finally a part of something that dealt even the smallest blow to PanTech, while helping the people of the village. However, the excitement was short-lived because the very next day, Ferris and I heard the news that the testing personnel had arrived and began mandatory registrations for the upcoming exams, and that meant us.

Arriving at the registration tent just outside the village, we found ourselves waiting in a short but very slow moving line. Everyone that had turned eighteen years old since the last time they came was here, and thanks to sleepyhead Ferris, we caught the tail end of it. Some of those standing in line looked overwhelmed with excitement and wonder. They couldn't wait to take the exam, and a part of me understood what they were thinking. If they'd never had personal dealings with PanTech, and didn't ask many questions, PanTech probably seemed like some kind of abstract, harmless manifestation of benevolent gods.

In reality, if it was a manifestation of anything, it was cruel and tyrannical gods who were only kind to those who obeyed and worshipped them absolutely. They hurt you for your own good; they'd say, to the twisted gratitude of their subjects. And, they weren't likely to be going anywhere anytime soon. I considered Lucille's plan. Even though there were problems, I was excited to think about how easy it might be under the correct circumstances. If she had been right in her assumptions about the commander, their armor, weapons, and the boundary, her plan might have actually worked. Or was I just dreaming too?

"I need more testing kits," the balding, bespectacled man in a white lab coat said to the soldier standing beside him.

"This is the last box," the soldier replied quietly.

"Last box?" he shouted. "I had twice this much ordered. What do you mean this is the last box?"

The soldier wasn't about to be intimidated by the man's shouting. "I mean this is the last box."

"Well, what happened to them? This is ridiculous. If I don't perform blood tests on these applicants, their transfer to PanTech could be delayed by as much as a week. This is an embarrassment."

A quiet sigh escaped the soldier's helmet. "They were stolen from our camp. Make do with what you have."

The man turned back around to the girl standing in front of him. "Alright, be sure to hold still. If we fail this test, I'm not sure I'll have enough to test everyone else here."

The soldier sighed again, but I'm fairly certain the overly stressed man in the lab coat didn't even notice.

I looked up to realize Ferris was staring at me with his brow furrowed.

"Taylor…," he started but thought better of continuing his sentence. Ferris was a lot of things but, stupidity is not one of them. Something on my face must have given me away—that, or the fact that I'd gone out at night without taking Ghost with me.

"State your desired post. Your exam will be tailored to your area of interest."

The woman stared down at her feet, hesitating.

"Go on. Don't be shy."

More silence.

"I know it's stupid, but can someone be a dancer? I told you it was stupid...."

"Dancer. Alright, testing for dancer. Don't be silly, girl. There are many dancers."

Wow. Dancers? Really? I had seen some cultural dancing in our village before, but not often. It was considered to be mostly a waste of time unless there was a specific celebration. Celebrations had gotten fewer and further between. I remembered that Mother's adversity zone had professional dancers. It made sense because the emperor was so pampered and surrounded by beautiful women whose sole purpose was to entertain him. What if this girl's request landed her into the servitude of the same sort of horrible human being? Then again, what was I thinking? It's PanTech. Of course, they're awful human beings.

He shooed the girl away and waved up the next person, a young man.

"Hold out your finger. You'll feel a small prick."

The young man complied, but it didn't seem to hurt him much.

"Soldier," he said.

"Well, I hadn't asked you that yet, but alright, soldier. I'm obligated to tell you that being a soldier is one of the more difficult positions to achieve. You must pass based on both intellectual and physical markers. Despite what you may think, the role of a soldier is one of the most revered positions in all of PanTech."

A loud cough came from the soldier behind him.

"Oh, would you shut up," the man in the coat said, turning to scold the soldier.

The soldier did not indicate how he received the man's remarks, hidden beneath his expressionless helmet.

"I'm sure. Soldier," the boy said, ignoring the apparent spat.

"Soldier, then. Next."

This continued with several others, until finally it was my turn.

"Sorry, I don't have any more tests for the two of you. I'm afraid you should've shown up earlier instead of dragging your feet," he said, adjusting his glasses. "All the same, choose your desired occupation."

"Test registration taker," I said.

He narrowed his eyes and leaned in. "Excuse me?"

"I'll get to sit at a table and be grumpy all day, right?"

The man started to open his mouth, but the soldier behind him interrupted whatever he'd planned to say with a loud and very unprofessional chuckle. Just one chuckle, but his helmet wasn't hiding this for him.

"Alright, if you want the most stressful and thankless job in all of PanTech—"

Ferris kicked me so hard in the back of the foot that I thought my feet were going to be swept out from under me.

"Alright," I said, bracing myself on the table to keep from stumbling forward. "Animal studies. I'm the veterinarian here. I want to continue researching animal medicine."

A lie, of course. I hadn't discussed my decision not to join PanTech with anyone and didn't plan to. I didn't want to have another argument with my mother or disappoint her. Ferris, too. I'd have to keep up appearances.

"Animal research. I've heard a rumor that the scientists there are about to begin some very exciting research. It is a rarely requested position, but perhaps it's the most ideal time to pursue it. Let's hope your brain is as smart as your mouth. If so, you should be fine. Next."

I stood aside and let Ferris step up. We really were the last ones to register. About time, too. I couldn't wait to get out of here.

"Desired occupation?"

"Soldier," Ferris said.

"What?" I breathed, so surprised that it's a wonder I was able to say anything at all. "Soldier?"

"Soldier," he repeated.

"But, Mother thought you'd want to pursue mathematics."

"I know. I'm good at it, too. Inherited the knack for it from Father, I suppose. Still, Soldier."

"Soldier," the man in the coat said, confirming. "I'm obligated to tell you that—"

"I overheard the warning earlier."

"I am obligated," the man continued, his eye twitching, "to tell you that the testing for the role of a soldier requires both intellectual and physical markers to be met. It is a prestigious position in the organization and is not easy to get.

You may be given a choice to transfer into a different position if you fail only the physical marker. No one is transferred into the position of a soldier unless they apply for it."

"That's a lie," I said.

The man's face turned as red as the commander's hair. "Girl, I'm about to have you removed from the testing. How dare you call me a liar?"

"Are you saying it's never happened? I know of a soldier who transferred to the position after his exam."

"For a soldier to transfer into the position after the exam, it must be because he excelled to such a degree that PanTech felt it would be such a monumental waste of opportunity not to place them in the position. Such individuals typically, receive high ranks and renown."

My heart sank, knowing that Linus resisted the system he was placed into. He renounced a road to power and fame.

"I'm sorry…I…just catch up to me, Ferris. I want to be alone for a few minutes."

I turned and walked quickly away, stopping between the tent and the village to wait for Ferris, wiping my eyes in hopes they'd be dry by the time Ferris came back.

A few minutes later, they still weren't.

Ferris caught up to me and hugged me tightly. "I understand why he didn't want that life."

"Do you?" I shouted. "It seems that you don't, since you chose it as your profession. Do you want to go around making things hard for children of other zones, taking away their food if they have too much, introducing predators if they're too safe? *Do* you understand, Ferris?"

He looked to the side, taking a deep breath before meeting my gaze again. "I do. I want to make sure there are as many sympathetic soldiers as possible. I want to be like Linus. Think about what would've happened if that giant snake had been set loose upon us, and there was no Linus to stand up to them and help you deal with it."

"Linus *died* doing that!" I was nearly screaming now, grabbing onto his shirt, before lowering my voice, remembering that we were out of hearing distance of everyone at the moment, but maybe not shouting distance. "I don't want you to die."

"I can do small things, Taylor. I don't have to be the big hero Linus was, but little things make a difference too. I'll be careful. I won't get myself killed or get into too much trouble, but I'll make a difference. The night he stayed with us, Linus told me many stories about things he'd done and gotten away with. There's a line, and you can stay just behind it."

Remembering what the commander said to me, I think I understood the real reason Linus got away with so much. The commander liked having him around. She didn't find him boring, and she found that…attractive…I suppose. I shuddered at the thought.

"You're a man, Ferris. You can decide. I'm sorry for judging you."

"It's alright," he said, "because I have something to say to you too. Consider us even after I do. I think you were involved in stealing the supplies. Taylor, *please*, if you're involved with the rebels, stop before it's too late. It won't end well. I could tell by how you were so relaxed and gave that sarcastic answer that you don't really plan on joining.

But, please, just think about it. We can make a difference, Taylor. You heard what he said. There's something major coming to animal research. What if you can influence that research to make a difference? So much of a difference that even PanTech can't stop it from helping everyone. Even Father would approve of that. Please, you don't have to say anything, but think about it. It's all I'm asking."

I didn't say anything. I'd already made up my mind. Even if I found a way to cure every disease and sickness known, make everyone immortal, and make rainbows show up in the sky every day, PanTech would still find some way to use it to harm everyone. They'd cure only those in their service, make their leaders immortal, and I'm not sure what they'd do with rainbows, but they'd find something. No, if I learned one thing from Linus, it was that no good could come from the inside. They needed to be destroyed from the outside. It was time to go speak to Ludo and the others and tell them I'd made my decision.

27

I didn't wait until nightfall. Instead, I walked directly into Ludo's shop, where he also lived, midday. I could estimate with confidence that's where the secret cave was located, so the blindfolding was more or less pointless. Then again, it might have actually mattered if Lucille hadn't revealed who furnished the cave, and who their leader was the moment my blindfold was removed. Lucille didn't seem to be the careful type, but bold and definitely smarter than she let on.

Ludo was occupied by whatever was on his workbench when I entered, and the bell on the door rang, resonating throughout the small room.

"Welcome," he said, still not looking up. "I've got some new boots in the corner over there, to your right, if you'd like to give them a look-over. Sized for men and women, and if I don't have your size, I'll make it in your size."

I humored him for a moment, walking to the corner without a word, glancing at the boots. Impeccable quality. Despite the fact Ludo was basically the only serious cobbler in the village, he didn't let that affect his sense of pride in his work. Even if there'd been a dozen others, odds were good he'd still be the best, and probably by no small margin. Hopefully, the same was true for me. I'd like to think so.

"You know, they're great, but I think I like the pair I'm wearing better. They fit like they were made just for my feet and legs."

He looked up and grinned, trying to hide his surprise that I'd just dropped in unannounced like this. "That's because they *were* made to fit your feet and legs. Cara's estimations were spot on. I believe I told you that you won't find a better pair for as long as you live, especially if you keep living here."

"It's funny you say that. Would you mind closing up your shop for a few minutes and heading into the back with me?"

He hesitated for a moment but obliged. "Sure, I'll flip the sign, and we'll head into the back. If anyone asks, I was showing you some of my new materials."

After flipping the sign and locking the door, Ludo led me through a door in the back and then through a hidden door in the floor under a table and rug. It was clever. The handle on the door was recessed in the door itself, so you couldn't see any suspicious shapes poking out from under the rug. The tunnel leading down was rough and unfinished, stone probably almost as old as the sand itself made one path forward, eventually leading into a larger stone space that opened up several times larger than the tunnel itself. The ceiling was taller than I could reach, but Ludo could reach up and touch it easily. I looked around and saw supplies lining the walls the whole way around.

I didn't understand, but I wanted to assume the best. "Why are the supplies still here?" I asked.

"We're keeping them," he said flatly and offered no hint of a further explanation.

"Wait…why? I thought the entire plan was to distribute these supplies to villagers in need. There's medicine here, and food and water. You could sneak these into homes where

PanTech has taken food away from children. The food's eaten. It's not like they can trace that back to us."

"Us? So, you've decided to join us then?"

I shouldn't have given him the opening to change the subject the way I had. That was stupid of me. Still, I'd be diplomatic and circle back to it.

"Yes, I've decided that I'm going to stay here in the village, regardless of my test results, and continue running the clinic and helping with our cause. Speaking of our cause, when exactly do you intend to distribute these supplies to villagers?"

"We're keeping them," he repeated. "What helped you to make your decision? Was the commander that rough on you?"

Another deflection, but memories of my interaction with the commander made me feel immediately uncomfortable.

"She wasn't so bad," I lied. "She agreed to amend her report about Linus. Not that it really matters. Probably just a trivial gesture to make me go away and give up my vengeful thoughts."

"And have you given them up?" he asked.

"No," I snapped. "I have not. Now, please stop dodging the question. Why aren't you giving these supplies to the villagers like you said you were going to?"

"Maybe I will, eventually. For now, they'd just go to waste. Think about it, Taylor. For the most part, they're just a bunch of PanTech worshipers. Doesn't that make them just as bad as PanTech, in just about every way that counts?"

"What? No...they're just afraid."

"Oh? How many of them stepped in to help your Linus when he needed them? You and he had just saved the village. He was their savior, and yet, all they could manage was to gather around and gawk as he lay dying on the ground. In fact, it wasn't until your Father learned about what happened that he came and took care of his body. Of course, PanTech dug him up anyway."

"They were afraid to help. PanTech soldiers would have stepped in and blown them to pieces."

He shook his head. "Then why should we give them what they were too afraid to take for themselves? Why shouldn't we benefit from the supplies? Swell our numbers? Expand our operations? Be better prepared to strike PanTech when the opportunity arises? Why risk being reported to help trembling idiots who are too afraid to even help themselves, and *still* find it in their hearts to thank PanTech for all the misery they inflict on their children?"

What was there to argue about? He was right, in a way, but although he was right, that didn't make what he was doing right. I couldn't come up with a rebuttal. I just stood there, thinking over everything in silence.

"Am I wrong? Not everyone is like you and me, Taylor. We don't need the weak around us clinging to us with their open hands outstretched, weighing us down, when our goal is to battle with the strong."

"You're not wrong," I said, finally. "I'm going to go. I have a lot to do today. I just wanted to stop by and check on the supplies."

Ludo looked at me, and something in his eyes felt untrusting. "Alright. Come by again soon. We should begin discussing our next move. We don't want to miss any opportunities."

I just nodded and left, making my way home. All I wanted to do now was check on Ghost and sit alone in my room for as long as possible.

It seemed I wouldn't be able to be the hero I wanted to be no matter what path I chose, and all those I thought might be heroes were never heroes at all, except for the only one I ever knew, who was now dead. My heart ached, thinking of him again. I wondered if I'd ever stop feeling his hand in mine and if his smile would ever fade. It seemed to only get clearer as time passed, but only anger could be found where fondness should be. As much as I loved him, I hated those who took him away from me more than that.

When I stepped through the door into my home, Mother was sitting at the table. She'd been waiting for me.

"Welcome home," she said, smiling.

"Thank you. I'm going to be in my room for a bit if you need me."

She patted the seat next to her. I knew what was coming, or at least I thought I did, and I wasn't really in the mood for it, but I obeyed and sat. I hoped I'd be able to brush her off quickly, though I immediately disliked myself for thinking that.

She reached out and grabbed my hand, squeezing it tightly. I jerked away quickly, my mind going back to the exact moment where the commander grabbed my hand as I was about to slap her. I gathered myself, took a deep breath, and placed my hand back on the table next to hers.

"Taylor? Are you alright?"

I shook my head. "I'm alright, Mother. Sorry. What did you want to talk about?"

She frowned. Clearly, she did not believe I was alright but didn't want to argue with me.

She was right, though. I wasn't alright. I was far from it and I wondered if I'd ever be alright again for as long as I lived.

"I spoke to Ferris when he returned. He wanted me to talk to you. *I* wanted to talk to you, and your father agreed to let me do it with just the two of us so you wouldn't feel ganged up on. I sent them out for a while to run some errands." She reached out and moved a strand of hair out of my eyes, and I again felt uncomfortable remembering my meeting with the commander. "We're really worried about you, Taylor."

It was always Mother's way to scold and demand, rarely to ask and be kind. She must have truly been afraid for me, for her to speak this way.

"I'm alright, Mother. Just…the exams coming up, and everything that happened with Linus, and having to lose sleep to go out and train Ghost…I'm just under a lot of stress, you know?" I lied.

"If you were in trouble, you would come to us for help, right? I always wanted you to see PanTech the way they ask us to see them, the way I saw them when they saved me from the awful life I was living because I knew that would make your life easier and make you less conflicted about your path forward in life. Now that I see that you're determined to think differently, I want you to know that I support you anyway, that your father and I love you, and that Ferris loves you too."

My fingers began to tremble without realizing it, and my vision became blurry with the tears that had started to flow. I flung my arms around her and released my pent-up emotions on her like a sandstorm.

"Oh, Mother. I don't know what to do anymore. I don't know what's right and what's wrong. I don't know who's good and who's evil. I can't tell the right path from the wrong one, and I hate...everything! I hate so much. I'm so angry. I want them to pay for what they did to Linus, but I still want to help people. I still see his face every day. Every time I close my eyes, I see his death, and I feel his kiss on my lips, and that wound, I see him dying, and it makes me so...angry, but so sad too. I...I don't know who I am anymore."

She wrapped her arms around me and stroked my hair. "Shh. It's alright. When you can't make sense of the world around you, always remember to trust yourself most of all. Don't believe what you see, or what you hear, if your gut tells you that it's wrong."

I nodded. My gut wasn't telling me much. All it wanted to do was tie itself into knots and make me feel sick. It didn't even want food anymore like a normal gut should. How was I supposed to trust that?

"Thank you. I think I'm going to go rest in my room for a while."

She nodded, moving her hand to my shoulder before letting me go completely. "That's good. If you haven't heard, testing is tomorrow. You should get some rest. Ferris said you declared animal medicine. I'm sure you'll make everyone proud, but make yourself proud first. Don't worry about what everyone else wants until you get what you want."

"Tomorrow?" I asked, surprised. I hadn't realized it would be so soon. Would Mother really not be disappointed when she found out that, even if I passed, I was rejecting the invitation and staying in the village? I was too tired to think about it anymore.

I went to my room, and in the privacy behind my closed door, told Ghost everything about what happened. It was somehow therapeutic to give the full, unabridged truth to someone who couldn't repeat it.

Exhausted, I quickly drifted off into sleep.

28

At last, the day had arrived. The day we were all told to look forward to, but filled nearly all of us with endless dread. The exam was extremely difficult to pass, and only a few passed each year. Sometimes, none at all. You only had one shot, and if you failed, you failed forever. There were no retakes. No do-overs. No second chances. Some were insane enough to revoke their admission into PanTech. The only person I'd ever heard of to do this was my father. A brilliant inventor who was dedicated to improving the lives of everyone in the village soon after barred from building anything that would reduce the adversity score of our village's children. If he didn't? Soldiers would have to create more adversity themselves to fill the gap. Confiscating food, sabotaging our drinking systems, or worse. Who wouldn't want to leave such a place to join a different world? A world of infinite technological advancement. A world without adversity scores, where it was decided that you'd already paid your dues and you could now live in comfort and luxury; scientific discovery and power, unlike anything any of us could even conceive of…and I'd decided to forsake it all.

Despite that, I still needed to do my best on the exam. Otherwise, what meaning would the gesture have? If I failed the exam and decided to stay, it would mean nothing. Leaving wouldn't be offered. No. I had to pass and throw the best score I could manage into their faces.

Ferris was up before me, as unpredictable as ever, and had made all of us breakfast, including Father, who was his usual quiet self this morning. He puffed on his pipe but wasn't reading or writing this time. Simply absorbed in an apparent daydream, which he was unable to escape from, save for the absolutely minimal effort required to lift his pipe to his lips and pull a few puffs from it.

"Father, are you alright?" I asked.

At first, he didn't answer, still trapped in whatever waking dream held him.

"Father?" I spoke again, louder this time, as I sat down at the table.

He heard me that time, smiling and nodding, before going quiet again.

"You seem troubled. Are you worried for Ferris and I?"

He sighed and sat down his pipe on the small leather stand in front of him. "Not worried. Just sad, I suppose, in a way. There's a chance that both of my children will be leaving forever, and I'll never see them again."

"Will you be upset if we join PanTech?" I asked, genuinely curious. It was a question I'd been wondering the answer to, but given everything that had happened recently, I hadn't had the chance to ask.

"Your mother and I discussed it. We've agreed that our personal feelings about this decision should be secondary to your own. We will support you, pass or fail, go or stay."

Mother walked over behind him and placed both hands on his shoulders. He brought his hand up and squeezed hers.

I'd prepared myself for uncomfortable questions from everyone this morning but hoped they wouldn't come. As we all sat around the table, eating our breakfast, tension filled my stomach, both with the anticipation of the upcoming event and knowing that these questions from my family could still come at any time. But, after we'd finished our breakfast and Ferris and I prepared our packs for whatever was to come, the questions never came. In fact, nothing ever came. Beyond my brief exchange with Father at the table when I first arrived, not another word was uttered.

Ferris and I continued to walk in silence slowly out the village and toward the tent set up for testing. There were two tents now, instead of just the one, and we soon found out why. Testing was divided among those seeking to become soldiers and everyone else. Soldier candidates would also be supervised by the commander and submitted to an intense physical trial. Ferris was lighthearted, but as all the young women in the village liked to remind me of frequently, he was also a physical specimen. He hadn't chosen a profession in the village, but he found enjoyment in hard labor. If something broke, he was first in line to help fix it. If heavy things needed to be moved from one place to another, he was happy to help. And, unfortunately, if someone were to call out for a young man to remove his shirt and be gawked at by all the pretty young women in the village…he'd probably be at the front of that line too.

As for me, I was happy that I wouldn't have to see the commander today. Though, I'd prefer it if it were never again.

We sat at desks, and a stack of paper was thrown down in front of us.

The same older man in the white coat and glasses from yesterday paced in front of us, his hands clasped behind his back. "This is going to take all day, perhaps into the night, so I'd advise you to get comfortable and begin thinking of how you'll resist complaint. This will either be the proudest or, for many of you, the most disappointing day in your life.

The majority of you will likely fail this exam. There is no shame in that. I wish only to instill in you a comprehension of the seriousness of each and every question.

"Each test has been tailored specifically to each of you, based on your declared focus of study. If you find that any questions are unfair, you are mistaken. If you find them to be too difficult, you are right. If you have any questions, that is too bad. I will not be answering them. Once you complete your exam, you will wait until everyone else has as well. Results are produced instantly. Curious how that is possible? If you pass, you will learn that and more, and if you fail, you will never know, nor will you ever need to know. Begin."

I opened the paper packet and held the first sheet up to the light, which drew an instant and intense glare from the man. Hoping to avoid any confrontations with him today, I gave up on that little experiment pretty quickly. Though I could've sworn I saw something woven inside the paper. This was no doubt some sort of PanTech advanced technology and had something to do with how the results were determined instantly. After I sat the paper back down in front of me, I could've sworn I saw the man grinning at his desk, still looking at me.

Two soldiers were in the tent with us, no doubt to protect those administering the tests from a potential rebel attack. Including the commander and assuming there was another soldier in that tent, meant that all available soldiers were preoccupied with testing. It's a shame Ludo and the others didn't know that. What a golden opportunity. One that would, no doubt, go to waste.

As I moved through each sheet answering questions, I couldn't help but be distracted by the thoughts of Ludo and what he'd done, or more specifically, not done with the supplies, and what he'd said about the other villagers. He'd lied to me. He didn't want to help the villagers. He only wanted to help himself. Helping them was just an unintended consequence if he ever helped them at all. Was this really any different from the hubris of PanTech? Then again, Ludo wasn't my enemy. PanTech was. So, it didn't matter.

I remained focused throughout the remainder of my exam, sure to give everything I had to each and every question, reading and rereading each one. I was prepared to take all night if I had to and make everyone wait for me to finish, but it did not come to that. To my surprise, I was the first to finish. I handed the man my stack of papers, and he only pointed to my seat in return.

For hours I sat, letting my mind wander to all the places it had taken refuge over the past weeks. Thoughts of Linus, mostly, filled my mind. I saw him everywhere, and everything seemed to remind me of him. I wondered if I would ever be able to go a day without mourning him, but I knew that such a day would eventually come, even if I didn't feel like it would right now. Time heals wounds, but not always. Sometimes time spreads them wide and allows things to enter and fester, only deepening the wound and making them worse. Even time couldn't be counted on.

At last, in the late hours of the evening, the final villager handed in their exam. Everyone had begun chattering amongst themselves, including the soldiers who stood behind the man overseeing the exams.

At first, I thought hearing Linus's name was just my thoughts echoing from inside my mind. I nearly dismissed it outright, but listening closely, even from the back of the line, I heard it again.

"Linus was supposed to be overseeing this. I had the night scheduled off," a male soldier remarked.

"Found a way to be a pain in the backside even in death. I'm impressed," replied the female soldier's voice.

"Yeah…truth be told, I miss him. Can't say the same for Peter. It's a shame that cobbler reported Linus. Otherwise, the commander would've never sent Peter and Oscar to collect him. He'd still be here, and I'd be back at camp enjoying some drinks."

My blood ran cold, and I froze in place. Every cell of my blood seemed to catch fire all at once, and I thought my skin might melt off my body or burst into flames too. The room began to sway, and I fought the feeling that I might faint. My mind collapsed in on itself, and the room went deathly quiet. I couldn't hear the soldiers, nor the villagers, nor the man give the results to each eager person standing in line. I didn't notice the excitement or the disappointment. I didn't feel the hurt in their voices or the life-changing happiness. I only felt rage, and it threatened to burn me to ashes.

I turned and started to walk from the tent.

"Where are you going?" the man shouted behind me. "You're not allowed to leave until everyone receives their results. Get back in line."

I ignored him completely, running from the tent toward home. I didn't slow down until I got to the door, where I took a deep breath and fought for the last shreds of composure I could muster so as not to alarm Mother and Father. I stepped inside.

"Welcome home, Taylor. How did it go?" Mother asked.

"Oh, I'll be getting my results soon. I was worried I forgot to lock Ghost's cage properly in the excitement of the morning, and the man overseeing the tests was nice enough to let me run home. I'm afraid I can't stay long, though. Sorry."

I didn't wait for an answer. I ran into my room and collected two of my knives. One I hid in my pack, and the other I stuffed into my boot. I looked at Ghost, who was noticeably distressed and spoke to him in a quiet voice.

"It's okay, my friend. It's likely I won't be back, but this is good news for you." I reached out and opened the door of his cage, and he tilted his head in response. I then raised the small window on the wall near my ceiling, just large enough for him to fit through. "I'm setting you free. Thank you for everything. Thank you for the purpose you've given me. For all that you've given me, and…and, I'm sorry. I love you, Ghost. May your hunts always succeed, and may your kills always be swift. But…maybe avoid foxes from now on."

I reached gently into the cage, hesitating at first, knowing one tiny drop of his toxin would paralyze me for a full day at best, but he didn't appear alarmed. I stroked his back, then turned, and left the room, my rage finally tempered by the sorrow that I'd never see my friend again.

29

Many were still outside their homes, waiting to comfort or potentially congratulate their children, their child's friend, or neighbor. It was impossible to be subtle right now, but right now was the time I had, and nothing was going to stop me from doing what I needed to do. But…what did I need to do? What did I want to do? I could sneak up behind him and bury my knife into his back, but more than anything else, I wanted to know why. Why, if he knew what Linus was doing, would he report him and set the events in motion that would kill him? He was helping me. He was helping the village. He saved so many and was willing to risk his life to do it. He had to pay. There was no forgiving this. There was no letting it go.

I stood in front of his door. I checked the handle. Locked, and the sign said closed. I hammered the wooden door with my fist. "Ludo! Get out here!" I shouted.

"We're closed; come back tomorrow!" he shouted in return.

I hammered on the door again. "It's Taylor. Get out here, now!"

I heard him unlocking the door and stepped back several steps to give myself distance. Ludo was almost triple my size, and there'd be no escape if he grabbed me.

He stepped outside, looking around at all the onlookers who had started watching us now.

"Can't this wait until tomorrow?" he asked nervously.

"No. It can't wait another second. Why did you report Linus? If you'd been watching us, you knew what he was doing. Why did you do it?"

He laughed, watching the faces of everyone around him. "I don't know what you're talking about. Go home, Taylor."

He turned to walk back into his house, and I threw my knife into his door. He turned around slowly, clenching his teeth.

"Because he was PanTech scum, Taylor. What more reason do I need?"

"Scum? He saved everyone from the giant snake PanTech brought. If you knew enough to report him, I know you knew about it! He was on our side. He risked his life for us. For you!"

"For me? When my father was dying and needed medicine, where was Linus when the soldiers refused to trade for it? Where was Linus when PanTech decided I'd had things too easy? Maybe seeing my father die an agonizing death would toughen me up. Well, it did toughen me up, Taylor. So long as he wore that armor, he was my enemy. We got three of them with one trick by pitting them against each other. That's a good start, but now you've gone and ruined all of that. All of our plans, all of our progress, all because you wanted to make a spectacle of everything. So, you've come here to kill me, have you? Here I am!"

He reached onto his belt and pulled out his knife, and I pulled mine from my boot. He took several steps toward me, but I held my ground, ready for any opening I could find.

He broke out into a run, holding his knife above his head. I held mine in front of me and braced the hilt with my other hand. If I landed the hit, it needed to go deep. I lunged forward and extended my arms, hoping my speed advantage would end the fight quickly.

But, the speed advantage I thought I had turned out to be wishful thinking. He blocked the thrust with his left hand, taking the knife blade into his palm, all the way to the hilt. Blood dripped from his hand onto the knife and my hands. He brought his knife down above me. I raised my leg and slammed my foot into the side of his knee, causing him to miss my neck, but the knife slashed deep across the back of my shoulder.

I bit into his right arm and held tight. I thought my teeth would come out as he tried to pull away. Out of the corner of my eye, I saw his headbutt coming, but there was nothing I could do. It was better than getting stabbed by the knife. The first hit gave me a false sense of confidence that I could take it, but the second one sent me to my knees, and I lost my grip on both his arm and my knife.

"Someone help her!" I thought I heard someone shout.

"But she attacked him first," shouted another.

"Hurry, get the soldiers!" another voice boomed.

He brought his knife down again, and I shot my palm up into his nose, sending him stumbling back a couple of steps, but he countered quickly with a punch to my jaw, and I thought again that I'd lose consciousness. Somehow I didn't, but it didn't matter. I felt dead on my feet. My arms were numb, and I couldn't lift them. My vision was blurry, and I swayed on my feet. Another punch hit me in the face, and blood poured out of my nose onto the ground in front of me, sending me stumbling backward. Only Ludo caught me before I could fall to the ground, holding both hands tightly around my neck, squeezing.

The shouting of the people around us intensified as the crowd grew. Several people tried to step in and stop him, but they weren't able to pull his hands free. Before enough of them could grab him, I saw the other rebels run out of the door and begin fighting them off. Even without knowing what was going on, they ran to their leader's aid. But, who was I kidding? They knew exactly what was going on. This seemed like a plan Lucille would come up with. This one didn't have any fatal flaws, it had worked. But that couldn't be right. Most likely, she would have never risked recruiting me, which could only mean one thing: She was unaware. This was all Ludo's doing, and he assumed I would never find out. I almost didn't.

All at once, his grip loosened. I choked and coughed as I was able to breathe again, all of my blood flowing into my head again. My eyes began to clear, and I could see what happened but couldn't make sense of it. Ludo's neck had a horrible wound, and blood ran down onto his shoulder. He was frozen in place. He faced straight ahead, his arms falling loose to his side. His eyes were full of fear as he looked around in horror, unable to process what had happened to him.

Wing beats boomed as the falcon slowed on his next circle around, and he landed down onto my arm, sinking his claws in deep. The blood from Ludo's neck slowed as he collapsed onto the ground. Lucille screamed and raised her knife, starting to rush toward me. Ghost beat his wings at her approach, and upon seeing him clearly, she immediately dropped her knife and fell backward. Cairn, who had been next to her, did the same.

"That's…," he started to speak but stopped and scrambled to his knees. "Oh, gods…," he said, clasping his hands together.

Lucille gathered herself and reached for her knife, but Cairn grabbed her arm.

"No. Don't you see what that is? This is an omen. The gods have spoken. Don't provoke their wrath, please," he begged.

I looked behind me, saw Heather and Lapis being held on the ground, and realized it was Mother who was holding them there. I hadn't even noticed she'd arrived. Father was standing behind her but was breathing hard enough that I could tell he'd only just caught up. Did Mother really disable both of them that quickly?

Before I could speak, the loud stomping of armored feet filled the momentarily quiet air with the sound of a new threat.

The commander arrived with two soldiers, as well as Ferris.

"Hah!" the commander bellowed. "You did it. You had me fooled. I never thought— What's that?" she asked, nodding to Ghost. "A new species for me to send to the university."

"No!" I shouted. "He's mine. He's staying with me. You said I could bring a native animal with me to study. This is it. I choose the shadowfalcon."

"First of all, girl, those aren't real…," she said, almost reflexively. "We've looked for them. What's this, some kind of cleverly disguised vulture? Second of all, how do you know you even passed your exam?"

I didn't answer, the blood from my arm stained the sand below me where Ghost's talons sank in.

"Alright, well…regardless, I keep my promises." She looked to the soldiers beside her. "Arrest these rebels, and the chieftain, for his incompetence. We'll find someone better to do the job this time. And this village used to be so well-behaved…." As she was walking away, she looked back over her shoulder. "Of course you passed, by the way. You'll be going to the university. You can take that…whatever it is, with you."

One of the soldiers flung Ludo over his shoulder and held the other rebels at gunpoint, ordering them to walk in front of him.

Once they were gone, everyone continued to stand around me. At first, I was oblivious, but after a few minutes, I realized everyone was waiting for me to say something. Several people had already gotten onto their knees and clasped their hands together, especially the older villagers, in reverence to Ghost. Do I speak honestly to them? Do I tell them he's just a bird and, even when I set him free, he simply reverted to his training? Only…I'd given him no command. Did I really believe what I'd been saying anymore? There was definitely more to Ghost than I'd originally thought. How much more, and what, I didn't know.

No, sometimes hope in a lie was better than no hope at all.

"Everyone…what you see before you is real. An omen of hope in a bright future to come. A shadowfalcon. He has chosen me to bring about this new future, and he will accompany me along the way. Better days are ahead, not just for the village but for the entire world. I'll be leaving soon, but I will never forget all of you. Please, be good to each other."

Once home, Mother tended to my wounds again. Ferris and I said our goodbyes to everyone. Cara apologized to me endlessly again for what Ludo had done. She hadn't known about any of it.

Five of us had passed the exam this year, including Ferris and the other soldier, but it was unlikely any of us would ever see each other again.

I was both excited to take part in this groundbreaking animal research and terrified at the same time of what it might mean. The events of the recent days made me feel as though the decision had been made for me by some…higher power, chance, the universe, whatever you'd want to call it. But I was going to make the most of it. Other heroes had made a difference in my life, and I would never forget them. It was time for me to become the hero of my own story.

PanTech, you'd better get ready, because I'm coming for you.

Epilogue

"Come on, it's not like you don't know how pointless this is to have as a vanity project. Put your own ambitions aside, and let the military take charge." The giant man ran his hand over his long, black beard, patiently waiting to see if his adversary would take the bait.

"Hah," the thin, bespectacled man chuckled. "Vanity project, you say? Ambition, you say? You are one to talk, General. Your post is as useless as you are, and your words are as hollow as the paper enemies you imagine. Why the president keeps you around is beyond my ability to comprehend. The project will remain with me, and if you speak to me with due respect, you will perhaps benefit from my research."

Struggling at his own game, the General clenched his teeth, fighting to maintain his composure. "The president keeps me around, Lab Coat, because I keep him around. I monitor every uprising attempt reported by every commander in my service, from the small but disciplined armies to the back alley riffraff. I know about it all, and I make sure it is dealt with swiftly and productively. And, don't forget, I make sure we stay prepared for another incident like we had a hundred years ago."

"Lab Coat? My, you are so, so very clever, General. You mean the eastern invasion? Be careful; you'll sprain your shoulder trying so hard to pat your own back. Not only was that before our time, but it was also an incident hardly worthy of note. By the way, 'Professor' would be far more dignified on your part, would it not? You wouldn't want your soldiers to hear you be so disrespectful to a man of high station, such as myself, would you? Imagine the scandal."

The General sighed. "I'll speak to the president…Professor. We'll see what he has to say about all of this. If the eastern invasion were such a trivial matter, then why are we still talking about it a hundred years later?"

"General, you are trying my patience, as I'm sure is your intent. At least you will find my agreement that you are indeed good at something. PanTech controls all territories on the planet now. There are no longer any independent, foreign territories. Who do you suppose will threaten us, some remote, indigenous tribe somewhere that we've somehow not accounted for? Really, you should be in charge of the College of Theater, not Adversity Management. Your flair for the dramatic is truly a spectacle worthy of marvel." The thin man flipped his blonde ponytail from his shoulder to his back, and despite his thinner frame, seemed to be enjoying his nearly full head of height advantage over the general a bit too much.

"Fine. Clearly, you have a lot invested in this project. After all, it is the single greatest possible advancement to the College of Animal Studies. I'd imagine it is frustrating for you, being a man of genius and so poorly regarded by our president, that you are relegated to animals, leaving the human studies to more capable men and women. And the purpose of the project? What a joke. How could you possibly take pride in creating designer pets? A man of your genius, cleaning out litter boxes and dog kennels all day?"

The blonde man sighed and pushed up his glasses. "General…while it may be true that you are the preferred lapdog of the president, you have whispered paranoia into his ear for so many years. But I'll have you know that because of my research, PanTech will mark one of its greatest scientific breakthroughs in the past fifty years. This will have an impact far beyond my dying day, which I'm sure you hope will be soon, and my name will be written in our history books and taught in our classrooms, while yours...well, for what purpose would yours be included? Wasting our resources on over-preparation for another invasion that will never come is hardly, *hardly* noteworthy, wouldn't you agree?"

"Without me, are you certain your name will be worth writing either? A designer cat, capable of saying 'hello' to his lazy, over-indulged owner, while impressive from a scientific standpoint, is not the sort of thing you remember who was responsible for. Now, take, for instance, war dogs that are capable of following and understanding commands. And—"

"Talking war dogs? Really, General? I thought you had no interest in talking to animals."

"You didn't let me finish, Professor. You want me to stop being so paranoid? Imagine the potential to monitor adversity zones if we were able to send in, say...a bird who could listen to conversations and report back her findings. A mouse, crawling beneath the boards of a home, who hears the very moment a man speaks to his family about creating any sort of uprising. You want me to be less paranoid? What better way than this? I'd no longer have to worry, knowing that everything was being effectively monitored and well in hand. No more surprises, like we keep running into. They aren't threatening now, but if you let any problem go long enough ignored, it will fester. Sooner or later, they will become emboldened and find a way to operate outside of our knowledge, *just* as they did a hundred years ago. However, this time, we'd know about it long before it mattered. We could all relax, but most of all, the president could relax. Don't you want him to focus more of his attention on scientific endeavors again rather than my military projects? This could be your way to earn his favor and set yourself up for approval of your future project proposals. How many of them have been turned down in the past decade alone, Professor?"

The professor sat quietly for a long time and began to gently tap on the wooden desk in front of him, his eyes locked with the general's.

"I'm not an unreasonable man, General. If you speak reason to me, I am certainly open to changing my mind. Let's say I accept your logic in this particular circumstance. What do you propose?"

The general removed his hat and rubbed his hand along his slicked-back hair, fixing the few strays that had begun to jut out.

"I'm so glad you asked, Professor. I saw the sparkle in your eye when I mentioned the animal spying idea. What if we repurpose your Animal Intelligence Evolution Project to this goal, ensuring PanTech is safe for many years to come?"

The professor shook his head. "No, I'm afraid I need to remain true to the original stated goal, which is to produce intelligent pets who provide a more complete companionship for their caretakers. If I change the scope of the project, I will have to apply again. If I do that, I risk being denied yet again, and even with your support, I simply cannot risk it."

The general sighed, tapping his finger on his chin. "I see...."

"However," the professor said, holding up his finger with a grin. "If we consider this project to have the true purpose of placing these intelligent pets in homes across PanTech, and, out of our shared interest in maintaining PanTech's goal of controlled adversity, we extend these pets to many homes within the adversity zones as well...."

The general grinned. "Thereby remaining true to the original stated goal of the project. I see. Professor, you are indeed as clever and capable as everyone says you are. I apologize for my earlier disrespect. Clearly, I have not spent enough time around you in person, and in error, I seem to have misjudged you."

"Likewise, General. I will offer you the same apology. Together, let us solidify the happiness of all PanTech employees."

"And the efficient control of all its citizens, guaranteeing we continue to become stronger through adversity," the general added.

The professor smiled and reached into his desk, pulling out a bottle and two glasses. "A toast?"

The general smiled to his new friend. "Of course."

After pouring the two glasses nearly full, the professor slid one toward the uniformed man who sat across from him, a symbol of his new respect.

"To friends?" the professor tilted his head slightly, his glass outstretched.

"To friends. To partners. To strength through adversity."

"Strength through adversity!" the two men shouted in nearly one voice, bringing the glasses to their lips and drinking the contents dry.

New Book Releases

Thank you for reading *Shadowfalcon*! This is the first book in the *PanTech Chronicles* series. We hope you loved the characters and the world of PanTech. If you enjoyed the book, please leave a review, we'd love to hear from you and we read every review!

Follow our authors on Amazon and Goodreads to receive new book release updates. You may also sign up for our newsletter at:

twistedkeypublishing.com

mrbrogath.com

Insurrection

Unleash the rebellion within! Join Taylor on a thrilling journey to dismantle PanTech from within, but she'll soon realize that her greatest adversary is herself. Prepare for an adrenaline-fueled ride into the heart of deception. Don't miss *Insurrection*, the second book in the *PanTech Chronicles*, and witness the relentless spirit of a heroine determined to change the world.

Others by M.A. Owens

Detective Trigger Series
Get *Mister Big* for free at mrbrogath.com/free

Others by F. Lockhaven

Short Stories

YA Fantasy Novel
<u>The Living Lore Series</u>

www.ingramcontent.com/pod-product-compliance
Lightning Source LLC
Chambersburg PA
CBHW020139120726
47903CD00007D/2332